The Forging of Finnian Ludwell

A.J. Prufrock

Standing Stone Press

ISBN 978-1-7362968-7-5 (Paperback Edition)
ISBN 978-1-7362968-3-7 (Ebook)

Characters and events in this book are fictitious. Any similarity to persons living or dead is coincidental and not intended by the author.

Illustrations by Molly Kantz

Editing and book design by Lucy Marsh

Printed and bound in the USA

Published by Standing Stone Press

For Will

Also by A.J. Prufrock

In Light of the New Moon

Walter and the Raven

A Circle of Dragons | Babiola

Oda's Warning   1

Ash and Beech   7

Lady Lost   16

Lady Found   21

Elia Asks a Favor   28

A House Divided   34

A Fit of Passion   39

Sir Dunstan and the Door   45

A Boat in the Stream   54

Unexpected Succor   59

Awash in a Fount, Drowning in Books   65

The Palace Comes to Life   73

Awakenings   80

Five Words   86

A Couple at the Fountain   91

A Pit of Shame and Shadow   96

A Vessel Upon the Ocean   103

Green Eyes in a Grass Hut   108

Brothers at the Forge   115

Doubts and Distractions   123

A Song for One, A Meeting of Two   128

Marble and Soot   134

Splattered All In Red   140

Sir Finnian Finds His Courage   149

Sir Dunstan Gains a Squire   158

Dark Knowledge Put to Use   165

A Proper Knightly Burial   172

Finnian Returns   175

Appendix 1   179

Appendix 2   207

Appendix 3   232

Illustrations

Clear, mournful, waiting eyes met his, peering from a face lovely and solemn, content and still. II

A lamp burned with a dim reddish flame and the head of a woman bent downwards as if reading. 48

Three walls were covered from floor to ceiling with ancient books. 68

Undiluted mocking peals of laughter rang against the cavern walls. IOO

In one hand he held a sword that shone with a dull fire. II7

Adorned in a splendid suit of armor, Sir Finnian took his leave. 83

Upon the platform sat a throne, high above the heads of the surrounding crowd. 94

Preface

THIS WORK IS A TRIBUTE piece to George MacDonald's *Phantastes*.

Written in 1858, *Phantastes* would have long ago faded into obscurity except for its impact upon the spiritual life of C.S. Lewis. Lewis recalls his reading of it—"That night my imagination was, in a certain sense, baptized; the rest of me, not unnaturally, took longer. I had not the faintest notion what I had let myself in for by buying *Phantastes*."

Long story short—without *Phantastes*, there would be no Narnia.

In my early twenties I shared *Phantastes* with more than one friend. No one finished it. In fact, no one seemed to get past chapter two. It bogs in the hands of a modern reader. Had it not been assigned reading in my undergraduate days, I would never have finished it myself.

Lewis, who says of MacDonald, "I fancy I have never written a book in which I did not quote from him," went on to criticize MacDonald's craftsmanship as "undistinguished, fumbling, verbose, floridly ornate, and over-sweet."[1]

This assessment is truer now in our century than it was in Lewis's.

But though MacDonald had questionable literary form, he was a man of unsurpassed imagination. *Phantastes* is a twinkling jumble of a dragon hoard. I have attempted to burn away one-hundred-year old dross to let the work shine again and hope I have at least made the story as exciting to today's audience as it once was to Lewis.

I owe MacDonald a great deal spiritually. He widened my world when it was quickly narrowing, collapsing in on itself. For all he gave to me, I want to resurrect his art by giving—in deep gratitude—all of my art to him.

I also owe a debt of gratitude to Aaron Mitchell whose insightful suggestions inspired this second edition and Lucy Marsh for her editing work done out of love.

A.J. Prufrock

---

[1] Preface to *George MacDonald: an anthology, 1946.*

I

Oda's Warning

A country maiden came towards Finnian from the depths as he walked through the forest. She offered no greeting and kept her eyes averted. The two came within a stride of each other but, instead of passing, she turned and walked alongside. Keeping her face downwards she busied herself with a bouquet of flowers freshly gathered. Not knowing what else to do, Finnian kept his stride. Not knowing what to say, Finnian kept his silence. Then, in a rapid low tone, the maiden spoke like a secret comrade deep in enemy territory.

"Trust the Oak," she whispered. "Here in Capgrave, trust the Oak, the Elm, and the great Beech. But be careful of the Birch, for though she is honest, she is young and changeable. You must shun the Ash and never trust the Alder. The Ash is an ogre—you will know him by his thick fingers. The Alder is beautiful but will smother you with her web of hair. She has only recently changed sides." All this was uttered without pause or alteration of tone. And then, with no chance for question or reply, the maiden took a hard left fork. Walking with the same unchanging gait she veered off into the forest.

It was the young woman's manner and remarks that convinced Finnian he was not lost in a dream of his own making. No such woman existed in his rich imagination. He had indeed gone to sleep in a book and come awake in its pages. The librarian had warned him, but he had not believed her. Certain volumes were not checked out for good reason, at least not to the likes of him.

The right fork in the wood, the one more traveled but not chosen by the maiden, brought Finnian that very afternoon to the backside of a small cottage. Just beyond the threshold, a woman sat preparing vegetables for the evening meal. As Finnian came near, she looked up but showed no surprise. Bending her head again over her work, she said in a low tone, "Did you see my daughter, Oda?"

"I believe I did," Finnian answered.

The woman smiled only slightly and stayed focused on her paring knife. Finnian stood before her dumbly, wondering if perhaps he was expected to move the story along. He chose a nondescript line from a play he recalled, hoping to engage without too much intrusion into whatever plot he had fallen. In stilted monotone he asked, "Can you give me something to eat, ma'am? for I am very hungry."

"With pleasure," she replied, but her tone stayed low and secretive. She motioned for him to come in with her finger to her lips, as if some ominous presence were listening in.

As Finnian crossed between the door posts she whispered, "The Ash is watching us."

Finnian noted the chairs and tables of cypress from which the bark had not been removed. The pieces were joined together with fine craftsmanship but the beautiful dovetailing was obscured below rough bark, as if the tree had grown new skin after being made furniture.

His hostess shut the door and put another chair before the already set table. Her hands were delicately formed, though brown with work and exposure. She motioned that he should eat. Finnian picked a bit of carrot from the pile being prepared for the pot. Finding it quite real and sweet to the taste, he made a request. "Tell me more, please, about the trees."

Before a word could be given in return, the shadowed limb of an ash-tree passed across the western window, bluish foliage appearing amidst the surrounding truer green. The woman jolted with impatient terror, bolted across the room, and blocked the little window with a decrepit old book.[2] It slid in her grip, creeping out of its binding as if desiring to escape. But she was determined that it should sit on the sill and shut out the majority of the invading rays.

---

[2] See Appendix 3.

"Usually," said she, recovering her composure, "there is no danger in the daytime, for then Ash is sound asleep. But today, all the trees are restless."

What is to be dreaded from the shadow of a tree? wondered Finnian within himself.

His hostess continued, "The trees sleep during the day. But when it grows dark, the Ash will be awake and on the hunt."

Before he could ask exactly what or who the Ash was hunting, the maiden he met in the forest entered. A smile passed between the mother and daughter but Oda spoke not a word. She did not sit or greet their guest, busying herself with small duties about the cottage.

"I should like to stay here till the evening, if you will allow me," Finnian said, "and then go on my way."

The woman stiffened as she gave answer. "You are welcome to do just as you please but it might be better to stay all night than to risk the dangers of the wood after dark. Where are you going and why the hurry?"

"I don't know. I suppose I'm eager to explore," Finnian replied. "I wish to see all that is to be seen. And you both have given me reason to think that a night in the woods of Capgrave is altogether different from the day."

The matron looked at Finnian and shook her head, "I'd call you a brave youth if you had any idea of what you were daring, but you are simply a rash one since you know nothing about it." She threw up her hands and breathed out a sigh. "Do as you wish."

Finnian wished to change the subject. He asked to see the old book which screened the window, and to his surprise, his hostess took it down. Before bringing it to him, though, she pressed her face against the pane and stared at the forest. She then drew a white blind down and over the sill. Finnian sat at the table where he had eaten and placed the old volume in front of him with care. Soon captivated, he read on and on, till the shadows of the afternoon began to deepen. Darkness encroached upon the forest, but Finnian did not notice until a low hurried cry escaped from between his hostess's pursed lips.

"Look there!" she hissed. "Look at his fingers!"

The setting sun shone through a cleft in the clouds piled up in the west, as a shadow of a large distorted hand with thick knobs and humps for fingers crept over the translucent white blind. It projected gnarled and knotted over the plastered wall and rough ceiling.

Oda noted just above a whisper, "He is almost awake, mother, and greedier than usual."

"Hush young lady, you need not make him more angry with us than he is. Your father is often obliged to be in the forest after nightfall."

Overpowered by fearful curiosity Finnian half blurted, "This cottage is deep in the forest! How are you safe here?"

"The Ash dares not come nearer than he is now," Oda replied, pointing to the oaks bearing up the four corners of the house. "They would tear him to pieces."

"Still, he tries to kill us with fright," whispered her mother.

The night continued to darken and the Ash continued his silent threats, stretching out his long arms and thick knobby fingers. In the shadows of moonlight he flickered and faded until a single clear moonbeam pooled on the floor unmolested.

In a low voice mother turned to daughter, "Oda, make haste—follow and watch. See what direction he takes."

Less than an hour later Oda returned with the news that the Ash had sped in a south-westerly direction. Finnian, if he was traveling east, could depart at once. This he did, for neither hostess seemed eager for him to stay, though they did pack him a parcel of food and asked his name to bless him.

The blessing of Aelryth and Oda carried him farther on his journey than he knew.

2

Ash and Beech

A S FINNIAN LEFT, it was dark enough for him to see that every flower along the path was shining with a light of its own. Tall lilies grew on both sides of the way and their large dazzlingly white petals glowed against the universal green of their foliage. The lamping foxgloves shot up their heads, peeped at him, and then drew back.

By the mossy roots of the trees, darker nooks wove a network of light and shadow. The glowworms lay in little tufts of grass, each dwelling in a globe of its own green light. Hovering overhead an interwoven dance of splendidly colored fireflies charmed each other, crossing and recrossing before flitting off into the trees. One or two were trapped in spiderwebs, a light dinner waiting to be consumed. Even the bloodthirsty spider glowed briefly.

Finnian's eyes could trace the course of the great roots into the earth where the sod was shallow by the faint iridescence that came through. Every twig, every vein on every leaf, was a streak of pale fire.

The further he went into the wood, the fewer came the warm sights and sounds. Instead fear encroached and tension wrapped round. As Finnian pressed on eastward, he strove to occupy his mind with other thoughts. What he feared he could not tell, and he had not the vaguest notion of the nature and tactics of his imagined enemy.

The clouds in the west had risen nearly to the top of the skies and were traveling slowly towards the moon. Their advance guard had already reached her and her beams waded through a deepening filmy vapor.

Then across the moon appeared the shadow of a large hand, knotty joints protruding on each knuckle. A sense of danger and a need for action sent Finnian dashing on and off the path, pointless in all his directions. He stabbed about for logical explanations, searching for the source of the bulbous reaching fingers. No ash tree was in view, yet still the shadow came moving to and fro like the claws of a wild animal. It clutched at Finnian with an uncontrollable longing for anticipated prey.

Nearing exhaustion and strung taut between helplessness and inevitability, Finnian caved and surrendered. The center of the clawing shadow lay within the open field ahead. Into its wide palm he threw himself, collapsed, rolled over spread eagle, turning his eyes towards the gazing moon. His mind froze with fear, anticipating death and nothingness as the hideous mass descended upon him. The phantasmic translucence in the center palm gradually deepened in substance towards the outside. Five claws were silhouetted against a horrible face that fluctuated and pulsed from an inward light. It had a curve-less mouth, colorless lips, a fixed and gaping jaw. Above the mouth were two voracious, unblinking eyes; alive but not with life, devoured by the heat of its own insides.

On the edge of blacking out, Finnian noted a cloud floating across the face of the moon. The obscured shine stole the shadow from the Ash, and, with his captor momentarily disarmed, Finnian broke free from the paralyzing grip. He sprang to his feet and scrambled away from the pursuing shadow-branches, bounding headlong into stationary trunks. He dashed himself about from tree to tree, bouncing to and fro against rough bark, freed from the pursing terror but lost in the dark.

Great drops of rain pattered on the leaves overhead. Thunder began to mutter and growl in the distance. A single flash of lightning gave Finnian a sense of bearings. On and on he ran as the rain fell heavier. At length the thick leaves could no longer hold up the deluge, and, like a second firmament, they poured their torrents onto the earth.

Drenched, Finnian came to a small swollen stream rushing through the forest. He quickened his pace, floundered across the water, and ascended the rising opposite bank. Here stood only great trees, free from saplings and underbrush. Successive flashes of lightning threw fresh shadows upon the earth, carrying with them that same horrible hand ever before him. Finnian was stung to yet wilder speed.

At last his foot slipped, and half-stunned he fell face first into the mire. Raising himself from his belly he involuntarily looked back.

The hand hovered within three feet of his face.

In that moment, helpless in the face of pursuant evil, Finnian felt two large gentle arms thrown round him from behind. He heard a voice like a woman's say, "Do not fear the monster, he dares not hurt you now." With that, the shadow-hand withdrew as from a fire, disappearing back into the darkness and the rain.

Finnian, overcome with the mingling of terror and joy, lay for some time insensible. When he awoke, it was to the sound of a gentle wind amidst the leaves of a great tree. It murmured over and over again, "I may love him, I may love him. For he is a man, and I am only a beech tree."

Finnian found he was seated on the ground, leaning against a human form. The branchy arms were the shape and form of a woman's. He did not move except to turn his head, for he did not want the arms to untwine themselves. Clear, mournful, waiting eyes met his, peering from a face lovely and solemn, content and still.

"Why do you call yourself a beech tree?" Finnian asked.

"Because I am one," she replied in the same low, musical, murmuring voice.

A.J. Prufrock

*Clear, mournful, waiting eyes met his, peering
from a face lovely and solemn, content and still.*

"You are a woman," Finnian returned.

"Do you think so? Am I that much like a woman then?"

"You are a very beautiful woman. Is it possible you should not know it?"

"I am very glad you think so. I feel like a woman sometimes, times like tonight—and always when the rain drips from my hair."Finnian remained silent and leaned his head against her trunk.

She continued, "There is an old prophecy in our woods that one day we shall all be men and women like you. Do you know anything about the prophecy in your region? Shall I be very happy when I am a woman? I fear not, for it is always in nights like these, dark and stormy, that I feel like one. But I long to be a woman anyway." Her voice was like a resolution ending a complex series of chords. Finnian told her that he could hardly say whether women were happy or not, and admitted the ones he knew were not. He could not help sighing when he confessed this truth. She felt the sigh, continued to hold him, and asked, "How old are you?"

"Twenty-one," he gave answer.

"Why, you baby!" said she, and kissed him with the sweetest kisses of winds and leaves. There was a cool faithfulness in her affection that revived his heart wonderfully, and Finnian feared the dreadful Ash no more.

"What did the horrible Ash want with me?" he said finally.

"He wants to bury you at the foot of his tree. But he shall not touch you, my child."

"Are all the ash trees as dreadful as he?"

"No. Though they are all disagreeable selfish creatures, this one has a hole in his heart that he is always trying to fill up. If he ever becomes a man, I hope they will kill him."

Finnian shuddered and gave thanks, "How kind of you to save me from him."

"There are some in the woods from whom I cannot protect you. But I will take care that Ash shall not come near you again. Here, cut some off." The Beech shook her long bough-tresses over him.

"I cannot cut your beautiful hair. It would be a shame," protested Finnian.

"Not cut my hair!" she chided. "I must tie some of it about you. Do not worry. It will have grown out before any of it is wanted again in this wild forest." And then she sighed to herself, "It may never be of any use again—not until I am a woman."

As gently as he could, while the Beech hung her beautiful head over him, Finnian cut a long tress of flowing, dark hair. When he had finished, she shuddered and breathed as one does when acute pain, steadfastly endured without sign of suffering, is at length relieved.

She then took the hair and tied it round him, singing a strange, sweet song—

I will show who you are to the world one day
but today you are only mine
Now that I know you are tender and young
I'm content to bide my time
All the world's sins are of envy and shame
From spring leaf to death in the fall
Remorse and Forgiveness walk hand in hand
or they do not walk at all.

She closed her arms about him again and sang on, but this time it was a language of the trees, and what little he understood of the first part was of no use to comprehend more.

The rain in the leaves and a light wind arose to keep her melody company and Finnian was wrapped in a trance of still delight. He fell asleep and knew nothing more that passed between them. He awoke to find himself lying under a superb beech tree in the clear light of the morning. It was just before sunrise and about his waist was a girdle of fresh leaves. The enormous boughs of the tree hung drooping around him. Leaves and branches above resonated with the song that had sung him to sleep, only now it sounded like a farewell.

With the sun well-risen, Finnian also rose. He put his arms as far as they would reach around the beech's trunk, kissed her, and said goodbye. A trembling went through the leaves, and a few of the night's raindrops fell at his feet. As Finnian walked away, he heard in a whisper once more the word—

> *I may love him, I may love him.*
> *For he is a man,*
> *and I am only a beech tree.*

3

Lady Lost

U PON LEAVING LADY BEECH, Finnian felt delightful refreshment entwined with a nameless sadness.

It is too bad I had to leave her sorry, the thought pricked in his conscience. Then he soothed himself. Perhaps I brought her what little pleasure she had ever had. Perhaps her life is now somewhat richer holding my memory. Finnian fingered the beech belt she had wound about him and sighed. If ever she is a woman, who knows? We may meet. There's plenty of room for meeting in the Universe. Self-comforted, he moved on.

Great treetops waved in the golden stream of the sunrise. Lights and shadows interchanged as leaf and branch swung to and fro in the cool morning wind. Three strong-armed beetles hurried along with unwieldy haste, awkward as elephant-calves. A large brown rabbit cantered slowly up and Finnian held stock still as the creature put one of its little paws atop his dusty boot. The rabbit looked up at the man with its beady black eyes and Finnian stooped and stroked it. But when he attempted to scoop it into his arms, it banged the ground in protest with its hind foot and scampered off at a high speed. It turned to look back several times at the man with appalled disdain before Finnian lost sight of its cotton tail.

Soon after midday Finnian arrived at a bare rocky hill entirely exposed to the hot sun. Not a tree was upon it, scarcely even a bush. His eye caught the depression of a natural path and began the ascent. Winding up through broken rocks, he was glad to find his course parallel to a tiny stream. Its waters were all that kept him from exhaustion in the heat. Just where the path seemed to come to an end, a large stone rose, half-closing a doorway to a cave. Finnian entered and was delighted to find a rocky cell with all its interior roughness rounded away. Mossy ledges like shelves were crowded with lovely ferns. In one corner, a little well of the clearest water filled a hollow. Finnian drank. He collapsed then upon a velvety mound that protruded from the corner like a couch, entranced for most of an hour. Revived somewhat, he glanced about, noting that each fern-covered shelf was decorated in intricate, spiraled bas-relief. He wondered who might use the place. Perhaps he lay in an artist's hideout, a haven where a sculptor might withdraw to set up his blocks of marble.

A sudden ray arrived through a crevice in the roof and lit up a small portion of the couch upon which he lay. It glistened. Fascinated, Finnian brought out a small knife he kept and removed a patch of vegetation. He found his bed was wrought of alabaster. He continued on with care since he found the stone was soft to the edge of his knife. When moss was removed from the majority of the stone bed's surface, he found it covered in complex curvilinear patterns and polished throughout.

As rays of sunlight continued to brighten the cave, a slight transparency was revealed. The translucent alabaster surface covered over an opaque white stone. A dimly visible human form was forged within the marble.

Gripped with anticipation and a startling sense of possibility, Finnian worked to remove all the moss as quickly as care would allow. Then he rose, stepped back, and beheld before him a block of pure alabaster enclosing the marble form of a reposing woman. She lay on one side with her hand under her cheek, and her face towards him. Her countenance was obscured by her hair which had fallen across her eyes with a single lock draped across her lips.

Finnian's fantastical encounter with the Lady of the Beech tree awakened wild possibilities. Might there be a way to awaken the beauty from her alabaster tomb? He knelt and kissed the pale coffin, but the lady slept on. Finnian sat on the floor and thought, rifling through every fairy tale he heard sitting on his mother's knee. If it was not a kiss that worked magic, weaving and unweaving spells, it was a song. Perhaps music could unbind and free the marble lady. Perhaps sweet sounds could go where kisses could not enter.

Though he always delighted in music, Finnian knew he was no singer. Yet the form of the woman was inspiring, and there was no other in audience to criticize and jeer. The little well had also proved an elixir and Finnian was about to discover that latent gifts were both awakened and heightened by its draught.

Filled with the courage that drink and women bring (and he had drunk deeply), Finnian leaned over the alabaster coffin. His face inches away from the head of the figure within, he sang. The words and tones came together and poured through him.[3]

As Finnian sang, he looked earnestly at the face so vaguely revealed. He fancied he saw, through the dim veil of the alabaster, a motion of the head as if caused by a sinking sigh. He dismissed it as imagination but sang out yet again.[4]

He paused. He thought the hand that had lain under the cheek had slipped a little downward but he could not be

---

[3]   *Wayside beauty now hidden out of sight*
I am drunk on the waters of thy tomb,
Thy form entrapped and shrouded from the light
My song calls out, "Awaken from the gloom!"

[4]   *Return to me O fountain of my life*
Curse be gone which holds thee in cold stone
Drink deeply from the torrent of delight
My heart calls out to thee and thee alone

sure. He began again for the longing had grown into a passionate need to see her alive—

Hope deferred, my heart grows spent and sick . . .

Then arose a crashing. A white form veiled in a light robe burst upwards from the stone. Like an apparition that came and left, she stood, glided forth, then flitted away out of the cave and down the hill. Finnian, stunned, his spent nerves making him slow, stumbled to the mouth of the cave. Cracked and broken alabaster littered the floor and hampered his blundering steps. He arrived only to watch her cross a little glade on the edge of the forest and disappear amidst the trees. Gazing after her he was hit by the despairing shock of having found, freed, and lost. It was useless to follow, yet follow he must. Finnian marked the direction she took and without once looking round to the forsaken cave hastened towards the forest.

4

Lady Found

A S FINNIAN CROSSED THE SPACE between the foot of the hill and the forest, his progress was interrupted. A horseman rode towards him and, from frontlet to tail, man and horse shone red in the sunshine.

When the knight drew near, Finnian saw that the whole surface of his armor was covered with a light rust. The golden spurs shone, the iron greaves glowed, the morning star which hung from the horn of his saddle by a heavy chain glittered with its silver and bronze. But the armor itself was unkept as if left out in the weather week upon week untended. The knight's whole appearance was warlike except for his face which had a deepening gloom tinged with shame. The horse, sharing his master's dejection, walked spiritless and slow. Even the white plume on the helmet was discolored and drooping.

The knight was riding past without looking up, noticing nothing but his own personal agony.

"Good day, Sir Knight!" hailed Finnian. The knight jerked up and drew his sword. When he saw the source of the greeting his face flushed. "Good day," he returned. His tone was of distant courtesy. He sheathed his weapon and continued on without slowing. Twenty yards out he reined up and sat still a moment. Finnian watched with some trepidation. The knight then turned his horse and rode back to where Finnian stood looking after him.

"I am ashamed," began the knight, "to appear as a warrior. The armor is just a guise now. I have been defeated by one with whom I had no business to tangle."

Finnian, not knowing what to say, stood and nodded.

"But since my defeat is no fault of yours, stranger," the knight continued, "I must give warning lest the same evil befall you. Take heed and beware the Maid of the Alder tree. I was proud but am humbled now. She is terribly beautiful—beware."

Before Finnian could inquire further, the knight struck spurs into his horse and galloped away. Finnian called after him, anxious to know more about this fearful enchantress and if she had anything to do with the lady he had awakened. But the knight heard nothing, shrouded in the noise of his armor.

FINNIAN CONTINUED ON HIS WAY, intent on finding his lost lady of the marble. A sunny afternoon died into the loveliest twilight. Great bats began to flit about in noiseless flight. The monotonous music of the owl issued from unexpected quarters in the half-darkness around him. The nighthawk heightened the evening's harmony with his recurring discordant jarring tones. Numberless unknown sounds came out of the dusk—dreamy and full of longing. Great boughs crossed his path, massive roots clasping the earth with all their might supporting monumental tree columns.

In the midst of the surrounding ecstasy Finnian forged through the twilight, sure that under some close canopy of leaves, leaning against some giant spindly stem, in some dank and mossy cave, or beside some leafy well, sat the lady of the marble whom his song had called forth. She sat and waited to be discovered, to meet and thank her deliverer. The whole night became one dream-realm of anticipated joy.

Remembering how his songs had called her from her prison, piercing through the pearly shroud of alabaster, Finnian thought, why should not my voice reach her now, through the ebony night that enwraps her? His voice burst into spontaneous song.[5]

Scarcely had the last sounds floated away when Finnian heard nearby a low delicious laugh. It was the laugh of one who has just received something long and patiently desired, a laugh that ended in a low musical moan, a laugh

---

[5]   *Return to me O fountain of my life*
Hope deferred my heart grows sick and spent
My heart knows well you hear and wait nearby
The veil between two lovers shall be rent

meant to be heard. Finnian turned sideways and saw a dim white figure seated on bent saplings in an intertwining thicket of smaller trees and underbrush.

"My white lady!" he cried, striving through the gathering darkness to get a glimpse of the form which had broken the marble prison at his call.

"It is your white lady!" said the sweetest voice in reply. A thrill of speechless delight shot through Finnian's heart.

Reaching her at last, Finnian took her hand in his and tried in the gathering darkness to draw close the beautiful face that had inspired his song. At the touch of her fingers a cold shiver ran through him. It is the residue of the marble, he said to himself, and heeded it not.

Then the lady pulled her hand away and would scarce allow Finnian to touch her.

"Why did you run away after I woke you in the cave?" Finnian asked.

"Did I?" she answered demurely. "That was very unkind of me. Forgive me. I did not know better."

"I wish I could see you. The night is very dark."

"So it is. Come to my grotto. There is light there."

"Have you another cave, then?"

"Come and see."

Her words were those of a lover but she kept herself withdrawn. She did not move until Finnian rose first, and then she was on her feet before Finnian could offer his hand to help her. She came close to his side and led him through the wood.

As they walked on through the warm gloom, Finnian reached to put his arm around her but she sprang away several paces. Alarmed, Finnian squinted to see her expression but could not in the ever-encroaching night. She returned to walk close beside him again as if nothing were amiss. He told himself not to judge. It would be unfair to expect warm relations from one who had slept so long and had been so suddenly awakened. Who knows what she might have been dreaming about lying in the alabaster? Her sense of touch might be exquisitely delicate.

After walking a long way in the woods, the pair arrived at another thicket.

"Push aside the branches," she said, "and make room for us to enter." Finnian did as he was told. "Go in," she said. "I will follow you." Finnian again complied.

He found himself in a little cave not very unlike the one of their first meeting. Instead of marble, though, it was draped with vines clinging to shady rocks. In the furthest corner, half-hidden in leaves, burned a bright rosy flame from a little earthen lamp. Lovely shadows leapt and mingled among the leaves along the wall. The lady glided in and seated herself in the corner, with her back to the lamp. Finnian beheld a form of perfect loveliness as the light of the rose lamp shone through her.

Enthralled by intense comeliness, Finnian lay at her feet entranced. The lady sat and chronicled for him a tale. She wove together snows and tempests, torrents and water-sprites, lovers parted for long years then reunited at last. The gorgeous summer night danced along as Finnian listened till he and the lady were blended with the tale, until he and she owned its history. They had met at last in this same cave of greenery while the summer night hung round heavy with love. The odors creeping through the silence from the sleeping woods were the only signs of an outer world invading their solitude.

FINNIAN WOKE as a grey dawn stole into the cave. The damsel had disappeared. He put his hand to his waist and found the girdle of beech leaves was also gone.

A shadow crossed the doorway and Finnian heard once more the low musical laugh of the evening before. But now it was full of scorn and derision. He looked and saw the loving gift of the Beech tree pulled through clenched fists. Long pointed nails shredded the Beech's hair with hateful hands. His lady of the evening before stared into the mouth of the cave. Then she said over her shoulder to one standing by, "There he is. You can take him now."

Finnian lay paralyzed, petrified with dismay and fear. He saw behind her the shadow of the Ash tree. His beauty was the Maid of the Alder and she was giving him as spoil into the hands of his awful foe. The Ash bent his Gorgon head and entered the cave. Drawing near, his ghoul-eyes and ghastly face stooped, his hideous hand outstretched. Finnian gave himself up to a death of unfathomable horror —helpless prey to a beast.

Just as the Ash was on the point of seizing with both of his gnarled hands, the dull, heavy blow of an axe echoed through the wood. Others followed in quick succession. The Ash shuddered and groaned with each repetition. He withdrew the outstretched fingers, retreated backwards to the mouth of the cave, then turned and disappeared among the trees. The Alder flowed after him wringing her hands and flinging strips of helpless bark—all that remained of the belt of beech branches. She looked back at Finnian once with a careless scorn-saturated dislike. Her molded features now putrefied by disdain, the Alder turned on her heel and vanished into the forest.

Finnian lay and wept. The Maid of the Alder tree had bewitched him—nearly slain him—in spite of all the warnings received from those who knew his danger.

5

Elia Asks a Favor

THE DAYLIGHT WAS HATEFUL TO FINNIAN. The great, innocent, bold sunrise seemed unendurable. The Alder's loathsome cave had no well to cool his face and his eyes burned with the bitterness of his own tears. Spiritless, he rose and walked towards the sunrise. He was distressed by his own folly but his greater anguish was over the perplexing question—how could beauty and ugliness dwell so near? Even now standing traumatized by the Alder's living-walking-faithlessness, even having just been deluded by her traitorous bile, Finnian was spellbound by the memory of her flawless physical perfection.

The question overshadowed even the pondering of his sudden deliverance, and the burning curiosity of whether or not the repentant knight had played a hand. Without the blows of the distant axe, Finnian knew he would have been dragged to the Ash's roots and buried like carrion, nourishment for yet deeper insatiableness. But at present he did not feel like one worth saving. He walked on and on, took intervals of rest, but had no cravings for food.

Spying in the distance a farmhouse, Finnian's heart was lightened to see a human abode. He hastened up to the door, knocked, and a kind-looking matron made her appearance. She gazed upon him as one who knew and said, "Ah, my poor boy, Aelryth sent word you might come in from the forest!"

The day before Finnian would have resented being called *boy*. But now he burst into tears at the word of motherly kindness. The handsome woman clucked and soothed. She led him into her home, made him lie down on a bench, and went to find him some refreshment. She returned with food, but Finnian could not eat. She compelled him to swallow some wine and this revived her guest sufficiently to pour out his distress.

"It is just as Aelryth feared," she said after listening in silence, "but you are now, for the night, beyond the reach of Ash and Alder. They cannot touch you here."

Finnian nodded feebly, then asked, "Can you tell me, ma'am, how is that Alder can be so beautiful without any heart at all—without any place inside even for a heart to live?"

"I cannot quite tell," said the matron, holding out a hand in introduction. "I'm Elia. Aelryth is my sister, Oda my niece." Finnian shook the firm grip and Elia began again, "I do not know much about the beautiful side of evil but I am sure the Alder would not look so winsome if she did not take pains to make herself so. Also you began your interaction with her as one in love. You mistook her for the lady of the marble. This gave her great advantage, for the kind of love you bore sees what it believes and disregards all doubts."

Finnian moaned knowing he had ignored all that did not fit his slavish desires.

Elia said, "Although the Alder loves no man, she loves the love of any man. When she finds one in her power she bewitches him and from his admiration she extracts her outward beauty. Men exude worship and she absorbs it as if she is indeed a goddess worthy."

Finnian moaned again.

"Yet," continued Elia, "The interior of the Alder Maiden — and I am loath to say this because she was once all glorious within—now wears away. One day the decay will burst forth and the lovely mask of nothing will fall to pieces. If she does not repent and keep repenting, she will vanish forever."

Finnian, ruing his own part in the tragic foolishness, did not hear the last of her words. But Elia's sorrow was not lost on him altogether. That night he wondered in his dreams if Lady Alder might have once been her bosom companion.

Elia rose to tend to other duties but paused to ask a favor, "During your stay here, Finnian, I ask you not say a word to my husband of your woes. He thinks anyone half-crazy for believing anything he has not seen himself. If you speak of Ashes, Alders, or ladies of marble, he will not allow you to stay under our roof. He is a good man but could spend a whole week in the wood and come back with the report that he saw nothing worse than himself, nor anything better."

"Of course, Lady Elia," Finnian said nodding. "I owe you at least that, and much more."

WITH ELIA BUSY ABOUT THE BARN, Finnian set himself in a straight-backed chair soaking in the ray of sunshine that poured through the kitchen window over an apron-front sink. The dining chair provided little comfort but it did not matter, for though he ceased to move, he was too agitated to rest. Here he remained in silent pensiveness until a jolly voice boomed through the open door leading in from the garden. Elia's husband called out in a husky tone, "Elia, the pigs' trough is quite empty! Swill them, lass! They're of no use unless they get fat. Ha! Heh! Heh! Gluttony is not forbidden in a swine's commandments. Ha! Ha! Ha!" Finnian liked the voice immediately, though he thought perhaps there was too much laughter.

The man's light joviality disrobed the room of its newness and disenchanted Finnian's daydreams with the tangibility of dirt and sweat. He now noticed the stacked dishes and spider webs that framed the window. The chair he sat in was not the arms of a beech and the rays of light through the window were not from fairyland. There the dust of a farmhouse floated and fell. Elia's farmer-husband entered and gave a nod in Finnian's direction accompanied by a grunt. It seemed that to him a stranger in his kitchen was nothing more than another stray cat that had wormed his way into the tender charity of his women. He drank straight from the faucet, pumping hard with his sunburned left arm, and ambled back out into the yard.

Not long afterward Finnian was fetched to join the family at an early supper. Elia's husband reached out to their guest and gave fat fingers in warm fellowship. His benevolent grasp matched the harvest moon of his affable face, wide and round like his ample torso. At his touch Finnian had no trouble suppressing his fantastical tale, for now he could hardly believe it himself. All at once he wondered if perhaps the ladies of both caves were only a wandering dream of a malformed imagination.

Finnian's fears of being asked for tales of his travels or intended destinations soon subsided, for the man of the house took no interest in his history or his person. Finnian was a guest with a new face and this meant to the farmer an audience with fresh ears. Elia's husband talked throughout the meal of pigs and hens, harvests and markets, rain and drought, fencing and barns. He rambled, smiled, and laughed a great deal. Best of all, he insisted on second helpings for everyone.

A daughter and son both in mid-adolescence sat on each side of their sire. The boy chortled and mirrored his father while the girl looked past all company at the table. She peered out the wide and open window and seemed fixated on the light tracing the garden flowers that wandered into the wood. Finnian looked too and saw that they planted themselves here and there along the path until the trees, thick and shadowy, blocked all possibility of new growth. When he next looked in the girl's eyes he remembered Ash and Alder, marble and Beech. The savory meal wafting in his nostrils and lying on his tongue faded as tree and leaf wove through his confused exhaustion.

6

A House Divided

SUPPER ENDED. Father and son retired to the hearth and beckoned their guest to join them. Tobacco and pipe were passed about. In time, the man of the house leaned in and queried, "The forest bears a bad name in these parts. I dare say you saw nothing worse than yourself out there?"

Finnian shook his head and blew a manly smoke ring.

"Ah! Then, perhaps, Heh! Heh! you will be able to convince my good woman that there is nothing very remarkable about our woods."

Finnian smiled and answered, "I certainly did see some things I could hardly account for. But I am a man in an unknown wild forest with nothing but the uncertain light of the moon to go by."

"Very true! You speak like a sensible fellow, sir, Ha! Ha!" the farmer laughed with a wide grin. "We have very few sensible folks round about us. Ha! Ha! My wife believes every fairy tale that ever was written and I do not understand it. Ho! Ho! She is a most sensible intelligent woman in everything else."

Finnian balked a little, feeling a vague sense of duplicity. "But shouldn't her intelligence make you treat her belief with respect, though you do not believe yourself?"

"Yes, that is all very well in theory," answered Elia's husband, puffing the pipe and tilting his chair back with an air of the superiority owed to age and experience. "But when you live every day in the midst of absurdity, it is difficult to maintain respectful diplomacy. Why, my wife actually believes the story of *The Ring of Doom* actually happened. Heh! Heh! Do you know it?"

"I read all those tales when I was a child, and know that one especially well."

"But, Father," interposed his daughter, turning from drying the dishes in the next room, "you know quite well that mother is descended from the elves. She has told us so many times."

"I can easily believe that," rejoined the farmer with another fit of laughter, "for her grey eyes and pointy ears. Ha! Heh! Ha!" In his laughter, the farmer's volume crescendoed into a loud bleating guffaw and then he bellowed, tears streaming down his face, "Always listening, aren't you my dear!" But Elia gave no answer. She heard his jest, but could think of no quip in return. The son, gaunt as his father was rotund, joined in the laughter, but his attempt at merriment transformed into a mocking sneer.

Elia returned from the barn, washed up, and served drink with an amused air. The men sipped and gulped and belched heartily. Finnian felt his traumatic adventure in the wood fade. Bygone and distant, his terrors and confusion were but a vapor of storytelling. Elia's husband joked, teased, chuckled, chortled, and roared. He took little note whether any of his audience was laughing along. His son continued to ape and echo his old man at every turn. Finnian was satisfied with his full belly and sat and smiled, only half-listening, with intermittent nods.

When the sun had been down some hours, the farmer stood, rubbed his belly, and tapped out his pipe. Looking at his guest, he asked, "In what direction are you going, son?"

"Eastward," Finnian replied. "Does the forest extend much further in that direction?"

"Oh, for miles and miles, though I do not know how far. For although I have lived here all my life, I have been too busy to make journeys of discovery. Ha! Ha! Nor do I see the point in wandering. It is only trees and trees, till one is sick of them."

IN THE MORNING FINNIAN AWOKE REFRESHED. He stood before the window in the attic guest room viewing the wide, undulating, cultivated country lit up with the morning sun. Various gardens—vegetable, herb, and flower—were growing beneath. Everything was radiant with clear, crisp light. The dew drops were sparkling; the cows in a nearby field were eating as if they had not eaten in days. Finnian, with no thought to alder or ash, went down to find breakfast.

Before he entered the room where father and son already sat and supped, he was met by the daughter. She had dropped her book[6] by the chimney-corner where she had sat keeping watch, and rushed up to catch him alone. Finnian bent his head as she tiptoed to whisper in his ear, "A white lady has been flitting about the house all night."

"No whispering, Ciara!" cried her father.

The sheepish pair entered the dining area together.

"Well, how have you slept? No bogeymen, eh?" the farmer asked in greeting.

"Not one, thank you. I slept uncommonly well."

"I am glad to hear it. Come and eat."

After filling their bellies, farmer and son went out and Finnian was left alone with mother and daughter. Elia and Ciara reminded him much of Aelryth and Oda but this house, Elia's home, possessed a persistent countering frivolity. Capgrave seemed under siege. Time spent there left no doubt that some measure of darkness was afoot.

---

[6] Ciara was reading a story from *The White Fairy Book* by Mme. d'Aulnoy. See Appendix 2.

Here in the house of Elia, a guest began to wonder if there was a shadow anywhere in the universe at all.

"When I looked out of the window this morning," Finnian said, "I felt almost certain that my days before arriving were all delusion. But whenever I come near either of you, I feel otherwise. I could be persuaded to never have anything more to do with strange happenings. Your husband seems content enough."

"Do you wish to forget?" asked Elia. "Do you wish to be as he?"

Finnian had no answer.

Just then from the yard came the call, "Send the young man out! We need his muscle. Ha! Ha!"

"If you work but an hour with my husband, all you saw with the marble lady will be no more," Elia warned.

"Then I must leave," said Finnian. "Let me gather my things."

7

A Fit of Passion

FINNIAN CLIMBED THE STAIR. Elia packed him a lunch and told her husband that their guest was leaving. The cry came up from the yard and reverberated in the roof and walls, "Room and board for free! Wandering miscreant!" The farmer's language grew foul and Finnian nearly went back down, cowed and submissive.

Ciara tugged at his sleeve. He had not noticed her following. "Come see my room before you go," she smiled. "It looks towards the forest." He followed obediently, the girl running before to open the door. It was a large room, full of old-fashioned furniture that seemed to have once belonged to a great house. A featherbed pressed itself against the sunlit corner, a chest of drawers opposite, but what Finnian noticed was the great picture window.

Through Ciara's window came a rush of wonderment and longing that flowed over his soul like the tide of a marvelous sea. The trees bathed their beautiful heads in the waves of the morning, while their roots were planted deep in the rich loam shadows. On the border between trunk and branch sunshine broke against the stems. The light swept in long streams through forest avenues and washed with bright hues all the foliage over which it flowed, revealing the rich brown of the decayed leaves and fallen pine cones. Finnian blinked and now the limbs were bare and burdened with snow gleaming in a winter moonlight. He rubbed his eyes and now instead of frost, buds burst light green from each and every offshoot straining from the tip of every branch. He watched until he could bear the beauty no more and then hurriedly returned to his waiting hostess.

Finnian bent in a low bow towards Elia where she sat churning the morning's milk. "Ma'am, you are right. I must bid you both farewell without further delay." Elia smiled and handed him a kerchief-wrapped meal. Then Finnian saw a mother's anxious look. Ciara had taken his hand. "May I put him on the right path, Mother?"

Elia nodded adding, "Only as far as the main fork, then straight back. Today's chores should not all fall to me."

NO LONGER HEADSTRONG, Finnian followed the young maid into the forest. She looked a year or two younger than Oda but carried herself as one older. The two scarcely spoke as they went along. Ciara led him through the trees then paused and reached into her apron pocket, producing a small globe. She looked at Finnian and then at the globe and her eyes danced. She was almost a woman but as she gazed upon the bright clear crystalline orb, her face was that of a fascinated child. Finnian could not tell if the globe was her plaything or her greatest treasure.

Ciara passed the globe from hand to hand, sometimes daring a short toss. Her manner vacillated between carelessness and focused anxiety. Watching her, Finnian took a great liking to her vivaciousness.

She looked up at him with a smile and tucked the orb away. They continued to walk but his curiosity grew. "Where did you get the globe?" he ventured.

"It is a family heirloom."

"Elvish?"

She shot him a look that nearly stopped him in his tracks but spoke not a word.

"May I see it?"

"No one but me is supposed to touch it."

Finnian held out his hand. She drew back, but he noticed a hidden smile.

"You must not touch it," she said with vehemence. Then, after a moment's pause she added, "Or if you do, you must be very gentle."

Ciara produced the polished sphere from her pocket and Finnian brushed it with a single finger. A slight vibratory motion arose accompanied by a faint sweet sound. Finnian touched it again, this time with two fingers, and the volume increased. When he touched it a third time with his palm a tiny torrent of harmony rolled out entering both of his ears with reverberations of beauty. Then Ciara placed her treasure back into the apron pocket, unwilling that Finnian should handle it any more.

They reached the fork in the path and Finnian's guide pointed his way. She turned to leave and he asked to see the treasure one last time. Ciara brought it forth and, as if glad to see them both, the crystal sphere began to shoot out flashes of many-colored flame, a loveliness irresistible. Finnian put out both hands and laid hold of it. A four-note chord resounded in a tempest of melodiousness as the globe trembled and quivered and throbbed between four hands. He had not the heart to pull it away but neither would he yield to her attempts to take it back from him. Regardless of her tears and pleading prayers he held fast, and the music went on growing in intensity and complication of tones. The orb vibrated and heaved until at last it burst in the air between them. A dark vapor broke upwards, turned, and as if blown sideways enveloped the maiden. For a moment Ciara was wrapped in thick shadow.

Ciara held fast the fragments remaining in her palms while Finnian let shards scatter at their feet, his hands dropping like dead weights to his sides. He stood paralyzed and aghast while the maiden gave a loud cry and fell to her knees, frantic to gather every splinter, trying even to catch them before they touched the ground. She picked and placed the shards, large to minuscule, into her apron pocket. Her motions were mad and frenzied as if the quickness might cause brokenness to reassemble into the beautiful, perfect, sacred, previous whole. She rocked back and forth several times, patting her pocket, moaning in trance-like prayer.

Finnian offered a kerchief and she accepted, wiped her dripping nose, and heaved three enormous exhaling sighs. He waited, lost as to what should be done next. Ciara threw the besmudged handkerchief down between his feet and fled from him into the forest, wailing like a child. A single accusing scream came echoing back, "You have broken my globe!"

Finnian, like one slapped, came awake and followed her. But he did not get far. His pursuit was met by a sudden cold gust which bowed every treetop above. A great cloud overspread the day and a fierce tempest came on. The wind in his face, he lost all sight of Ciara. With no heart to sustain the chase he cowered in the shelter of a hollowed-out oak. His spirits scraped the ground like the shards. His confidence in all his doings was shattered. His ears rang with the sound of her cry, "You have broken my globe!" He was filled with loathing for them both.

Finnian knew the globe was broken by his impulsive passion. He knew Ciara was gone and would not return. He did not know how to find the marble lady who captivated his very heart. And he did not know that the shadow of the broken globe, the dark vapor that had enveloped the maiden, had not followed her as she fled weeping. It had wrapped instead around the bark of the oak in whose trunk he now fitfully fell asleep.

8

Sir Dunstan and the Door

T HE NEXT MORNING, A SILENT FLOOD OF EASTERN GOLD flowed through every byway in the meandering woods. From between the trunks came a glorious knight. He was the same knight that had given Finnian warning, but he was much changed. He still rode the chestnut steed and his face was still sad. But his countenance pointed towards hopefulness, like one exiting rather than entering a mournful tunnel. His armor did not shine half so red. Instead it bore the blows of mighty sword and axe. The stain of shame had been plunged into the torrent of mighty deeds and was all but washed away.

This time he saw Finnian and reined his horse to a full stop. Looking down from his saddle, his hand lifted in a silent salute which Finnian returned. The knight beckoned him to travel alongside; otherwise aimless, Finnian followed along in agreement.

The two travelled together for days as Finnian's affinity for him grew. It was plain the knight suspected Finnian's missteps and weaknesses, but he asked no questions. For this, Finnian began to love him. Though Finnian saw the noble once or twice looking anxiously his direction, shame prevented speech. Neglect of the better man's warning, and a horror at his own deeds, caused him to shrink from even alluding to the cause of his gloom.

On the evening of the sixth day the two reached a split in the path. To the right chimney smoke billowed over the hill. To the left the path narrowed, a thicket on each side. Finnian leaned right. The horse was reined left. The two men looked silently at each other and understood there was a looming parting of the ways. The knight dismounted and took off his gloves. He put out a bare hand and Finnian took it into his own.

"Dunstan," he said, a late but heartfelt introduction.

"Finnian."

"Well, Finnian, before we part, have a cold drink with me in the name of friendship."

"Long overdue, Sir Dunstan," Finnian replied, smiling.

From his saddlebags, Dunstan pulled a flask and pressed Finnian to drink first. Finnian knew as the first drop touched his tongue that he drank once again the clear water from the little hollow tucked in the corner of the marble cave. His eyes brightened in thanks. The water's coolness roused his heart with deep feeling for his noble companion. He desired to fall on Dunstan's neck and confess to him the whole ignoble story of the Alder, not to seek advice—for that was hopeless—but for comfort and sympathy. Finnian opened his mouth to speak, raised his hands in gesture, and there spied a wound in his left palm. A splinter of the crystal globe, less than a quarter-inch long, lay imbedded. Its redness and pus brought to mind a second and deeper shame. The light in his heart grew cold and he held his peace.

Dunstan took his turn to drink deeply from the flask, wiped his mouth, and put on his gloves. The two parted.

No shadow followed the knight into the darkness of the thicket, but one floated high over the head of Finnian. It wafted from a treetop perch, lower and lower the nearer he came to a long, squatting hut. One end butted against a single tall cypress which rose like a spire skyward.

FINNIAN QUASHED A VAGUE MISGIVING and approached the half-open entrance. He saw a lamp burning with a dim reddish flame and the head of a woman bent downwards as if reading. An irresistible attraction caused him to enter without knocking but once over the threshold, he held stock still. The lamp was the only light source in a windowless room and Finnian could see the dim outline of a bed huddled in the corner. It and the chair the woman sat upon were the only signs of domesticity. Otherwise it was no more than a rude outbuilding used for storage. Several rough utensils lay strewn about.

A lamp burned with a dim reddish flame and the head of a woman bent downwards as if reading.

The woman never raised her face, but as soon as Finnian stepped in, she began to read aloud in a low drone from an ancient little booklet which lay open in her lap. Other than lips and tongue, the only movement in the dank room was the turning of a page, now and again, in the dark musty volume. She showed no notice of her guest, though he now drew quite near to her. Her face was sallow, her forehead high, and her black eyes recessed far into the sockets of her skull.

Between the chair and bed and directly under the lamp was a door of oaken ply, cracked and peeling. Finnian could not tell whether it was an opening to a cupboard or an entrance to another room.

Without lifting her head or looking his way the woman spoke in a whisper, "You had better not open that door." She then went on with her reading, part in silence, part aloud. The prohibition greatly heightened Finnian's desire. He hesitated, but was already lost.

Unused to resisting any heartfelt inclination, he crossed the room and in one motion pulled the door open to its full width. He looked in. At first he saw nothing worthy of his attention. It appeared a common closet. Shelves on each hand held little necessities: a bobbin of silver thread, a half-empty cask of rancid lamp oil, a sealed tin of hardtack. In one corner stood a single broom, half of its bristles eaten away by vermin; in the other corner there was a hatchet. There were no shelves on the back wall. In fact there was no back wall at all, just an empty space beckoning further in. Finnian again crossed a threshold and again held motionless. The woman's drone fell to just above a whisper while sinking to a bass note lower than he thought possible for the female voice to intone.

Turning back towards the room to spy whether another had joined her, his eye noted instead a dark form clinging bat-like to the lintel of the hut's entrance. An onslaught of horror and guilt wafted over him as he recognized the same thick shadow he had seen encompass Ciara as she held her broken globe. The shadow, with a shiver and great swiftness, rushed past the woman and wound around Finnian's face and neck. The door of the closet slammed in its wake. On came a tumbling tumult as the black creature entangled its host. Both fell down through the void of the missing back wall into an empty space, headlong towards the remote end of what seemed to be an underground shaft.

On and on they fell, scraping and skidding, undeterred by Finnian's clawing efforts to both free himself from his assailant and somehow slow the fall. Panicked and nearing a state of unconsciousness, his body landed with a thud against a second door of oak. His ears and nose told him oak; there was no light any longer. His breath knocked from him and most of his senses as well, Finnian at last regained his footing. He felt about and met nothing but cold earth on all sides but one. There was no choice before him but the entering of yet another door.

Finnian turned the creaking handle and pushed with all his might against rusty hinges. He expected a long narrow climb out of a pit deeper than any cellar, basement, or crypt dared be dug. The fall had felt like fathoms. But when the door gave way, he found himself with single step back in the same room, lit by the same rosy lamp, occupied by the same dark-eyed woman. Only the shadow was missing. Nothing clung to his neck and chest. Nothing hung from either threshold.

Finnian, eyes darting about expecting to be leapt upon once again, blurted, "Where is it? What is it?" He pulled at his hair and looked for pity towards the woman, who still sat reading.

"There, on the floor, behind you, clutching at your heels," she answered, pointing with her arm half-outstretched, but not lifting her eyes. Finnian turned all the way round and looked, but saw nothing in the gloom. Yet he could not escape an undeniable third presence. He stepped closer into the glow of the rose lamp and turned his head and neck to look back over his shoulder. There on the floor lay a black shadow the size of a man.

"What is it?" Finnian said, with a growing sense of horror.

"It is only your shadow binding himself to you," she replied through pursed lips. "I told you, you had better not look into that closet."

Now for the first time his hostess lifted her head, displaying a mouth full of long, pointed, white, shining teeth. He did not, could not, speak. He turned from her and left the cottage. His new companion followed behind like a dog.

THE SUN WAS HIGH ABOVE, and in its glow Finnian's shadow lay even blacker. He was bewildered—stunned—both by the event itself and its suddenness. He could still hear, if he strained his ears, the distant singing of Sir Dunstan just a few miles away in the thicket. He realized then that, in the blink of an eye, he had chosen not the companionship of a valiant knight but a constant strange attendee.

Finnian made his dreary way through the forest, the outline of his wretched shadow sewn to his heels. Even in sunless thoroughfares the two left traces of withered lifeless grass and scorched shriveled flowers in their wake. Only once did Finnian glance back to see what was strewn behind, and shuddered.

Now and then he tried to outpace his counterpart. Once he tried slowing to see if the shadow might leave *him* behind, to no avail. At night, it blended in with the surroundings. Come morning, it sat waiting. Several days in, he addressed the dark silhouette directly, daring it to do its worst. His shadow sat unresponsive and unfazed.

Though at first he was sorry for the grass and flowers he passed over, the shadow's melancholic presence eroded all resistance. In time all sense of pity wore thin and the wonder of the forest faded into ashen indifference.

9

A Boat in the Stream

FINNIAN'S SHADOW NO LONGER REMAINED AT HIS FEET. It rode along nestled in his breast pocket as its host wandered listless and directionless, feeding upon grubs and grasses, nuts and berries. When the sun set, Finnian laid his unkempt head down on whatever spot he found himself. Food and sleep was all that guided his footfall. The white lady seemed now a picture in a childhood storybook, the Lady Beech a figment of childish imagination. Eventually they entered his mind no more.

Finnian had entered Capgrave by a book. Men of his disposition, whose temperament easily slips down between the lines of Byzantine chant set in iambic pentameter, do not fare well when all sense of wonderment and mystery die. And when truth and beauty vanish as well, directionlessness turns to purposelessness in a blink of an eye.

His eyes glazed. He did not notice the trees thinning, foliage dying off, grass gone from green to brown to no more, stones ground to gravel underfoot. He did not notice that he had grown thin and gaunt and did not distinguish the present desert from the past verdure. He was sunburnt and did not feel it, thirsty and did not know it, starving and heedless of the empty grumble.

When cognition was on the verge of collapse, a small spring burst from a sun-heated rock.

Finnian noticed the anomaly.

A cool fountain trickled slow but steady. Finnian stooped and drank, lips to stone, then sat down beside it and cupped his hands beneath the flow. Finding himself refreshed, an affection for the water arose in his heart. His sun-scorched brain heard it warble a little tune.[7]

He sank his index finger into the mud beside the little fountain and drew several lines radiating outward from the trickle. As if choosing, the water filled only one of the finger-dug trenches, flowing faster like someone had opened a valve below.

Finnian excavated more in the direction the aquifer had selected until water overflowed his workmanship. I will follow and see where the water takes me, he thought, rising and sauntering after what had become a little rivulet, carefree and thoughtless as a child.

---

7 *I will flow, I will flow*
Come and see where I go
All your wounds I will lave
Rest upon my gentle waves
It is so, it is so

So down Finnian went with the current, over rocky lands burning with sunbeams. He saw only the shining water.

A few blades of grass appeared on its banks, and here and there a stunted bush dared grow. He saw only the dancing wavelets.

Half a dozen times the stream disappeared altogether underground. Not dissuaded in his pursuit, Finnian wandered about in the direction it seemed to take, remembering childhood games of hide-and-seek. He would smile in wonder when he found the brook and heard her sing once more. Again and again, the water would conceal herself. Again and again Finnian would find her, sometimes far away to his right or left among new rocks. He exulted afresh each time at the renewal of watery melodies. Green along the banks increased with the flow. Other streams joined in, flowing eastward on and on, and after many days' travel Finnian found himself resting by the side of a broad river.

A glorious horse chestnut tree towered above where he sat, dropping its blossoms, milk-white and rosy-red, all about. The river ran deep, an unfathomable soul. Torrents and eddies had hollowed out a wide gulf but now subsided into fullness like motionless sorrow. A gush of joy sprang forth in Finnian's heart and overflowed in his eyes. His powers of language, for lack of use, could not explain why, even to himself.

Wiping tears away, he took note of a little boat on his side of the shore lying unfastened. He waded through the brush to the brink of the bank. Stepping into the vessel, he pushed away from shore and out into the current. There he drifted, not caring that there were no oars on board.

He lay down, cradled in the hull. The whole skyscape glimmered overhead. In bewildering loveliness the sun sank over the great river twisting, twining, and flowing half-asleep like a glistening serpent. The least movement of the cargo sent wavelets out from the hull, heaving and falling into peaks and valleys of molten silver, breaking the image of the enchantress moon into a thousand fragments.

In passing clouds, illumined by moon and milky swathes of stars, Finnian saw figures forming one by one: the woman of the beech tree, Sir Dunstan, Aelryth, Oda, Elia, each standing alone. There was Ciara when she was whole and happy and delighted in him, and soon after the face of beauty in pale marble. It appeared and lingered, and Finnian thought he could be content forever for one glimpse of the light of her eyes. He felt he would cease to be for one word of love from her mouth.

With this thought the twilight sank around him, enfolding him into a deep sleep. He slumbered as he had not for months. The boat moved forward on a silent path beneath a round silvery moon. A second moon reflected up from the floor of the vast blue watery deep.

Come midnight Finnian sat up to see gigantic forest trees which slept about him in undefined massiveness. A strange melodious bird took up a song—a continuous strain that did not chirp and repeat but deepened with intensity like a coming farewell.

The birdsong faded like ripples of dying laughter. There came a great silence. The river bore the little boat round a bend with a gentle sweep, and before him rose a broad lawn lifting straight up from the water's edge. Its long green slope was crowned by a stately palace, ghostly in the moonlight. White marble reflected the moonbeams back making it seem to possess a light of its own. Dotted between stately columns, dark windows absorbed the pale light as it vanished within, absorbed by carpet and curtain.

Finnian loosened the plank that had served as his seat, paddled the boat to the bank, and stepped ashore.

10

Unexpected Succor

F INNIAN'S FEET SANK INTO THE SOFT TURF as he climbed up the bank. Cresting the hill, he turned to say goodbye to his vessel but found his faithful craft hidden in the shine of the water. Before he entered between the ancient posts where massive gates must have hung at one time, he looked towards the river once more. The boat was gone.

Continuing through the wide doorless gateway, he crossed a courtyard where a high fountain of red marble threw up a lofty column of water. Its spray fell in a fusion of sweet sounds into a basin beneath. The overflow ran in a single stone-cut channel towards an inlet east of the double-hung front entry. Following the stream, Finnian stepped upon pavement of interspersed white and red marble cut as diamonds. The door opened. He called a soft hello, hoping someone might answer, yet glad that no one did.

The vestibule was supported by tall white pillars. Though Finnian could see no one, hear no one, he felt a sense of welcome, as if behind one of the innumerable columns was someone who loved and waited for him. A sense of security saturated his mind and body and drowsiness came crashing down. The lovely cold marble hall, for all its beauty, was no place to sleep.

Finnian felt himself led by invisible hands up the corridor and down a darkened hall until a little white lantern shone over a single door of ebony. Silver letters upon the portal formed the words *The Chamber of Sir Finnian.* Well, he thought, hesitating as he opened the door, I have no right to claim the honors of a knight. But any doubts as to whether he was right to enter were soon dispelled.

A fire of applewood, supported by andirons of silver, was burning on the hearth. A bright lamp stood on a table on which were set his three best-loved books,[8] among them *The Ring of Doom.* Beside them, upon a large plate of silver, at perfect temperature, was his favorite meal. All comforts stood at attention like hosts awaiting a guest's arrival.

After filling his belly heartily, he sat long by the fire meditating. Wearied with thinking, he crawled into the comfort of a warm bed and floated into oblivion listening to the falling waters of the fountain just outside his window.

---

[8] See Appendix 1.

A.J. Prufrock

IN THE LAST HOURS BEFORE DAWN, Finnian threw both feet over the edge of the goose-down mattress and glanced out the window. On the sill was a ring of keys gone unnoticed the evening before. Next to the ring a lit taper threw its flame, like a flickering finger giving direction. It cast a pointing shadow over an old secretary desk standing silent on the western wall, made of the same solid ebony as the bedroom door. Each drawer and cubby glimmered with a central brass lock.

Finnian took the ring and with keys jingling in his left hand walked across the aged carpet to fit key to lock. He unfastened each drawer top to bottom and found them empty, until he bent over the last and lowest. Feeling a strange mingling of reverence and curiosity, as if the dead were drawing near to look over his shoulder, he turned the key.

At last the lock opened. One of the rusty hinges cracked and fell jangling on the floor. The little drawer opened, disclosing a chamber swept clean except for the corners. In one rear corner lay a little heap of withered rose-petals, all scent long since departed. In the other, tucked away, was a small packet of papers, tied with a bit of purple ribbon. A deep and wordless perception told Finnian these items were ancestral. Heritage and bloodline, physical and spiritual, lay within this small space. Past and present, inclination to ill and good, each emanated from the ebony family heirloom. It was identical to one he had seen sitting in his great-grandfather's parlor that had been passed down for generations. How did it come to be here?

Finnian pulled in a deep breath and exhaled heavily. The puff of air revealed the contents' fragility—rose leaves broke apart and parchment disintegrated. Reduced to a dusty cloud, fragments shrouded the small opening like a mist.

Finnian blinked through the powdery fog. He blinked again. Out of the drawer stepped in miniature form the marble lady his song had roused to life. A diminutive Greek statuette, she wore a simple flowing garment which hung from her shoulders and descended to her feet. All was white but the woven purple band around her neck and a matching one which gathered the garment about her waist.

Finnian was overcome with the presence of beauty. He reached to touch.

"Foolish boy," she said. "If you touched me, I would hurt you."

With her words, Finnian awoke into the full morning.

"FOOLISH BOY, FOOLISH BOY . . . " echoed in Finnian's head. But there was no lady, no secretary, no keys. Now wide awake, he found only the impressions of four ball feet in the thick carpet and a single rose petal brushed against the base board. Previously quite happy to be alone, he now felt despondent.

What made such a dream manifest? he wondered. Was this wakefulness now but a dream? When would he stop being a boy, and a foolish one at that? His aunt and father had wrung their hands over his impractical bookishness. Had he ever distinguished between real and fairy tale? Would manhood end the sudden bursting tears which led into trances of speechless delight? The fits would peak and leave him faint and longing for more, like a yearning to dance to beautiful music played just out of earshot.

Perhaps, once again, he was too much alone. Dreams within dreams wove through his reality making him unsure of his own wakefulness. He recalled and considered Elia and her unbelieving husband. If she did not have a daughter like Ciara who heard the music too, would she feel the unnerving isolation?

He wished now he had poured out his heart to Sir Dunstan. The noble knight would have given him guidance and true company. The blind now led the blind, and one of them carried a shadow in his front breast pocket.

Finnian shoved aside his sorrows and moved to the one other perceptible piece of furniture in the room besides the bed—a wardrobe. Inside he found a suit of fresh clothing. It fit him to the last detail both in size and style. The realness of the woolen weave brought him solace as he rubbed small imperfections between his thumb and forefinger. Little blemishes soothed and grounded him. Flaws were not the stuff of dreams.

Finnian now took stock. He recalled the little boat upon the river bringing him to this very place. He perceived that the magnificent palace had expected him to come, and knew him—the clothes, the books, the food were meant for him. The silver letters upon the door seemed to say a better Finnian was yet to come, or had already come but was not yet discerned. Not asking, he had received. So far nothing yet had been asked for in return. He was both comforted and perturbed.

Finnian's shadow had tempted him to fear and passion —and had succeeded. It had caused him to doubt long-known sources of delight and wonder but these now seemed poised to return. Unsoiled as yet was his sense of gratitude. But gratitude often nestles in the doorway of deserving.

II

Awash in a Fount, Drowning in Books

HAVING DRESSED HIMSELF IN HIS NEW FINERY, Finnian went out to see more of the palace. The hallways shone like silver in the sun, shafts of light streaming through every window. A thought of his shadow crossed Finnian's mind but he did not look round to see if even here it dogged him. He could not bear to rob himself of the pangs of beauty shooting through his heart. Yet underneath his childlike wonder pressed hard unspoken hope. If only I might find the light that would devour my hideous shadow, he thought.

A breakfast awaited him in a little atrium off the main hall. How it appeared there and by whose hand he could not tell, but he ate it with a thankful heart. Satiated, he continued to explore through the central set of hallways and amid them found a sunroom with a pale opaque ceiling of blue spangles. Constellations of silver stars were supported by pillars of a pale red. He marveled that all the silver in the house showed not a sign of tarnish.

Below the starry ceiling was a great basin. It seemed no bigger than the fountain in the grand entry but when he stepped up on the jutting base of its pedestal and peered in, the interior extended deep and wide, pressing out on all sides like a magnificent sea.

Without second thought Finnian stripped himself of his new apparel, folding each piece with precision and care, and placed the neat stack in a tiled alcove where a mosaic danced with mer-folk. He dove in. With open eyes beneath the surface, Finnian beheld wondrous caves hollowed out by ceaseless billows. There grew sea-weeds of all hues with corals glowing between. Creatures of all sizes and shapes swam alongside him, a few close enough to touch but most at distances too far to recognize their forms.

When he rose to the surface, he expected to be miles from land, leagues from the palace, swimming alone upon a heaving sea. But his eyes emerged from the waters and above him was the blue spangled vault and red pillars all around. Again and again he dove in and found himself in the heart of a great sea. Again and again he surfaced for breath and found himself in the palace fountain.

At last, exercised to the point of fine-tuned exhilaration, Finnian scampered out with ease from the water lapping against the brim of the sunroom fount. Tiny ocean waves spilt over the black marble border as he dressed and went out deeply refreshed.

As HE CONTINUED TO EXPLORE, Finnian began to discern faint, gracious human forms here and there throughout the palace. Some walked together in earnest conversation. Others strayed alone. Some stood in groups, as if looking at and talking about a picture or a mosaic. None of them heeded him. He felt no threat nor danger. He felt invisible, as if he were the phantom and they the real with both feet in the solid world. His fingers ran over his tweed jacket to moor him again and again.

His heart filled with gratitude for the artistry of light and shadow, the fountains and lovingly prepared meals, the quiet, and even the company that was not quite company. For many days he explored the palace no further, content to swim and read, eat and sleep. Then, in an absent-minded stroll down an unfamiliar corridor, he found the library.

Finnian stood in the doorway and stared about. Before him was a mighty hall lit up from above. The vaulted roof was crowned in a single piece of glass, stained throughout with a mysterious, fathomless picture in many splendid colors. Overhead were etched the same intricate spirals and complex curvilinear patterns he had last seen in the marble cave.

*Three walls were covered from floor to ceiling
with ancient books.*

He exulted and he balked. It was by a library that he had entered into the land of Capgrave with its trees and shadows and deep otherworldliness. Would he exit by a library as well? Would he return to the land of his upbringing, or would he discover a portal yet deeper still and lose his inborn senses altogether? He stepped in but vowed not to partake. To lay on the floor among the volumes would be enough.

Three walls were covered from floor to ceiling with ancient books. The fourth's full height was lined by silken curtain. The drapes descended from the vaulted ceiling in a stream of bright colors. The fabric gave no hint to what lay beneath or beyond.

Just the presence of books was calming. The paper smelled the same in this world as in the one from which he came. Finnian roamed aisle after aisle running his fingertips along the spines. As he strolled through the grand space he never removed a book, simply caressing the bindings.That night he slept like a babe. The next day he returned. And the next.

On day three, Finnian pulled out a work at random just to read the inner flap. The weight of a book, the texture of parchment, belonged in the world best known and oldest to him. In a great act of asceticism, he returned the volume to the shelf, satisfied that he could stop the urge at will. To prove further his powers, he opened a different work, caressing the table of contents. His hands shook this time as he returned it to its place.

The fourth morning Finnian went straight to the library after a rushed breakfast. He counted his strides from the doorway to the center of the room—forty-two. Now, guided by the cold science of mathematics, he felt safe to count volumes clockwise from the doorway, hand height. Opening the forty-second volume, he read the introduction and stroked the dog-eared corner of the forty-second page. Book re-shelved, he wandered to the back corner of the great hall. There sat the only chair and desk of the whole wide space. Also there peered out the only window within a wall of the entire chamber. It was clearly built for staring out. Enough light poured forth from the masterful ceiling for discerning the most faded, minuscule print.

Through the window Finnian spied a distant tower. It leaned slightly towards the palace, as if peering over the property it was built to guard. Its back was turned to forgotten threats over far horizons. Spread between the ancient lookout and Finnian's point of view rolled royal orchards and lush gardens. He gave no thought to who tended them and how often. They were but props to his copious fantasies, footing for the feet of fairies, shade for the ogres that chased them.

An hour later, he left for lunch trembling and happy.

After his meal, Finnian returned and counted books *counter*-clockwise from the doorway, hand height, choosing again volume forty-two. This he perused simply to get a sense of the writer's style.

On day five, Finnian gave himself over. Also the next day. And the next. Besides a brief breakfast and a swim in the sunroom fountain, the library was his abode. Here, day after day, he threw himself on one of the many sumptuous eastern carpets and scanned, and skimmed, and read. He managed with immense discipline to return to his room each night in great weariness. The library carpets were lush and soft and could have served as his bed, but the glowing silver nameplate called to him, and it could not be denied.

The books of the palace proved beyond all his past experience. Each volume was an experiential portal beyond all former daydreaming. If it was a book of metaphysics Finnian opened, he had scarcely read two pages before he was pondering over unfolding mysteries as if they had leapt from his own mind. If it was a book of travels, he found himself the traveller. New lands, fresh experiences, and novel customs rose around him. Finnian traversed. Finnian discovered. Finnian fought. Finnian suffered. Finnian rejoiced in his successes. Was it a book on history? Finnian was the chief actor therein. He suffered for his own faults. He was glad in his own praise.

With fiction it was the same. He took the place of the character who was most like himself and the story became his own. He acted out whole dramas, striding across the library floor with deliberate steps through entire epics. With grand gestures he paced along the silken curtain, voice and gesture changing to fit the role of a co-conspirator, antagonist, or lover. Lives full of years were condensed into an hour. Finnian would arrive at his deathbed at the end of a volume, looking up in sudden bewilderment to the consciousness of his present life and location. Recognizing the walls and roof around him he found he joyed or sorrowed only in a book.

12

The Palace Comes to Life

SOMETIMES, IN THE HEIGHT OF PASSIONATE READING, Finnian ventured to sing. He never gave voice to more than a few bars before an inexplicable shrinking fear would silence him. The few notes he sang made him astonished at the beauty of his own voice as it rang against the spines. Entrancing verses arose within him as of their own accord, crescendoing to fortissimo, full of themselves and their own melodies.

But when he sang quite softly, it seemed he could hear something like the distant sound of dancers.

One afternoon Finnian went to the library but took no book from the shelf. Literary adventures had been for weeks the reason to rise from bed. But today, he felt worn and thin. He could not assimilate another word. The thought of a single line of text brought a wave of queasiness. Instead, like the day he discovered the room, he ran his fingertips along a curiosity—not the walls of books this time, but along the wall of colorful drapery.

By stride forty-two he became conscious that behind the curtain was, and had been all along, the source of the sounds of dancing feet. Lost in literature he had found no drive to explore anything but his inner world, but now that he was beyond sated, he approached the curtain. He lifted its corner to find a long, high, and wide black hall, still as death.

There, under a great crimson globe high in the center of the hall, was an innumerable assembly of white marble statues. Men and women of every form were set before him in multitudinous postures. They loomed life-size in the ruddy glow of the large lamp, each upon a pedestal of jet black. Etched in golden calligraphy around the rim of the great light shone the barely legible words *SING WHILE YE MAY BUT TOUCH YE NOT.*

A peculiar delicious odor pervaded the place. Finnian felt a stronger than usual impulse to sing but held his peace.

Each statue, posed with the marbly stillness of thousands of years, had an air of motion as if just ceasing from movement. Each possessed an invisible tremulousness as if they anticipated Finnian's appearance and had sprung from the living joy of the dance to the death-silence of an isolated pedestal.

Finnian passed all the way through from one end of the hall to the other, discovering as he went that his first glance behind the curtain had been but an antechamber. He now traveled through a series of hallways and ballrooms, strung together like jewels on a tangled necklace. Each room had a grand pattern in the tiling, a mosaic guiding the steps of the dance. Each space grew grander and more ornate and colorful. As he traveled and studied the human forms, Finnian found that though all were white and perfectly still upon black platforms, each statue was unique, its own person. By the time he reached the tenth and final grand space, he had lost track counting the frozen population.

Finnian could take in no more and dragged himself back towards the library, ready to find his bedchamber and its promise of sleep. As he crossed back over the midway point in room five, he began absentmindedly to breathe the first line of the song that woke his marble lady.[9] As the lyrics escaped his lips, the statues moved. Ever so slightly, but it was undeniable.

Or was it? Finnian had been too long alone. His confidence in his five senses lay in tatters. Too long had he adventured with only his shadow as company. Too long had his only companions been in the pages of books. Finnian clapped his hand over his mouth to stifle all further music and began to run. Had his loneliness come crashing into his reality? His broken psyche was creating illusory companions and he could not bear it.

Frantic fear took hold when he heard, or believed he heard, a single soft pair of light steps patting after him.

____

[9] *Wayside beauty now hidden out of sight ...*

His legs pumped wildly. He did not turn and thought only of a singular goal—reaching his room and barring the door.

Finnian's objective was uncomplicated and his pursuer was lagging in the chase, but the silken curtains were his downfall. They hung limp and passive from the high ceiling as always. Calm mind and good form would have passed through like a gentle night breeze but Finnian's mad sprint was not in good form. Flailing in fear, his body became a tangled, thrashing cocoon. Mummified in bright colors, with arms bound tight, his legs continued beating against the marble floor. Close and closer his pursuer came upon easy quarry. The silk was pulled back from his eyes and he looked up at the figure leaning over. It was Oda. The maiden in the woods who gave warning stood above him. He was no longer alone in the large, lonely palace.

THE GOAL OF REACHING HIS ROOM was met at last, but instead of being alone, he sat in front of a fire beside real flesh and blood. There was so much to say that they began with a long silence. Finnian's usual meal was waiting, but this time he split it in two. It was, as usual, more than enough and the fellowship of sup took the sting out of a surprise guest. Finnian did not know where to begin. How much of his story did she know? How much did she need to know?

He considered pouring out all as he did with Elia. It was pleasant indeed to have another human next to him, breathing, eating, feeling the warmth of the fire. But unlike Elia, Oda was not the age of his mother or grandmother. She was a youth with no more experience than he, maybe less.

Accidental wisdom began their conversation at the point of shared experience.

"Did you see the statues move?" he asked.

Indeed she had and nodded, eyebrows raised slightly.

A pang of joy shot through Finnian. The unbelievable happening was confirmed by another. He could have kissed her for that simple confirmation. But, as quickly as it came, the joy was displaced by a sense of intrusion. He had perceived the palace as his alone. Had *she* been also been fed her favorite dishes by invisible hands? Was *her* name engraved in silver upon her door? Had *she* swum naked in the fountain? Here his mind stopped exploring. Oda was not ugly but she was no beauty.

Until his embarrassing entanglement in the silken curtains, Finnian had not known Oda was present among the marble statues. What else had she stood by in the shadows and seen? His sacred places were changed somehow by invasion of the other.

Oda was not a fairy or an elf or an ogre or a sprite. She was just as common as himself. When one mortal enters alone, the land of mermaids and fairies is a wondrous adventure. But Finnian felt the magic divide, not multiply, knowing there was another. Who else was staying in the palace? And, more pressing to his mind, who got here first?

All these tangled thoughts he pressed aside. He hoped, if given room, she would reveal more of her story. Most women broke under silence.

Oda seemed unnaturally comfortable in it.

"Have you seen the statues move before?" he queried.

"Only tonight when you sang."

Finnian's soul rested in the beautiful word—*only*. The music was his.

"I wonder what would happen if I sang the entire song . . ." he began.

"I think you should be careful in your eagerness for music," she cut him off. Finnian was taken aback by the curtness, especially from one who had up to now been so taciturn. Her tone had a biting undercurrent for which he could not place the source.

"How long have you been here?" he asked as gently as he could manage. Then, trying to lighten the mood, added, "How long have I been here for that matter?"

Oda shrugged. Finnian pressed, "Did you see *me* come? I certainly did not see you enter."

"I think we should sleep," Oda replied. "Come to my room tomorrow evening."

"Your room? I do not know which hall."

"You shall find it because now I want you to."

13

Awakenings

THE NEXT MORNING FINNIAN DID NOT FIND his breakfast placed by the hearth as he had grown accustomed, but a note instead which stated, "Breakfast is in the kitchen. Follow your nose."

And he did. A pot of porridge bubbled on the stove. Bowls were stacked, butter and sugar were out along with dried fruit and nuts. Finnian served himself and ate heartily.

Lunch was an invitation to self-service as well. Cheese and bread were hidden in a cupboard but he found them and savored each bite.

He did not swim that day. He had become too self-conscious to strip down. He did no reading either. Books were no match for a living breathing soul after going so long without, even a bristly soul like Oda's.

As soon as the sun began to set, Finnian set out for Oda's room, taking her at her word that he would know where to go. Beyond the servant's quarters, at the most eastern end of the smallest wing of the palatial manse—in what now happened to be the darkest room, far from the setting sun—he found her door. By candlelight he saw the silver inscription: *The Lady Oda.*

Finnian knocked but once; Oda opened and led him to her hearth. Both sat still and quiet, then she began, "I arrived a week before your little boat washed up. I was not ready to speak to you and kept myself apart. There are many wondrous rooms in the palace to explore. Our paths could have stayed separate much, much longer except for the marble statues. I go to be among them often, for somehow they comfort me. Then you gave them motion . . . "

Finnian's brow furrowed. Oda continued, "I cooked your meals and took them to your room. Your movements were predictable and it was simple to slip in and out unnoticed. The recipes and ingredients were delivered in a basket. Someone loves you, someone more noble than I. It was good for me to join in serving you for it has helped me to forgive."

Finnian's furrow deepened. He sat in a silent stare.

"For the broken globe, Finnian . . . my cousin . . . " Here the sure voice of Oda stuttered and she bit her lip.

Finnian now missed her cloak of silence.

He looked to the floor and stammered, "The meals were delicious. Thank you."

The short quiet space seemed long.

Oda went on, "You asked my opinion about your singing. And I have been mulling it over."

Finnian had forgotten but was glad for another topic.

"I think it is quite possible that your music breaks a spell. But if we make a purposeful attempt we might unleash more consequences than we can predict. Neither of us knows the reason for the marble statues' enchantment. We do not know if they are limited for their own good or a great calamity has befallen them."

Finnian was surprised at how glad he was to hear the word "we." He pondered a moment before answering, "You are right, presumption is a grievous error—just because we can do something does not mean it should be done. But passive cowardice is just as wicked. How can we not liberate captives if it is in our power to do so?"

"The only instruction given us is *don't touch*," replied Oda. She then added, her eyes twinkling, "I don't think sound waves count."

Finnian was glad to find a sense of humor under the blunt exterior.

The sun fully set. The pair left the quarters of Lady Oda and made their way to the labyrinth of halls behind the library curtain. What they planned to do together was daunting but the testimony of two witnesses brought courageous sanity to the unbelievability of what was anticipated. Finnian was too frayed after his long isolation to brave the undertaking unescorted. Oda's pragmatism anchored his more mystical nature.

Though he found fellowship in the sense of adventure with Oda, Finnian held as his own one unshared ambition: he hoped to find his beautiful marble lady among the statuary. If he did not find her, perhaps an awakened figure would have word of her, or know of her. Surely the marble enchantment here in the palace throng touched her lonely story in the cave. He had seen none in the palace encased in alabaster, but he felt sure music was the antidote to their paralysis. He had seen, and joyfully Oda bore witness to, the effects of a single line of lyrics. What might a whole song do?

In the marble hall, he had sung in passing, without forethought. In the marble cave the song had come upon him without effort. Conscious striving would not just be unavailing but counterproductive. Finnian knew that if his soul was not still, the music would not come, for this kind of music could not be found in seeking. It found you.

When the curtain lifted and Oda looked to Finnian to begin, it was thinking of the Beech tree that finally freed him from himself—the memory of her self-emptying forgetfulness. When he thought of her now, he knew that she would have loved any man in need of her succor because it was her nature to love. Her love had nothing to do with his ability to give or to receive. When his thoughts were all Beech—and self all but disappeared—the power of the song came, soft and low. It rang through his chest, throat, and lips and stirred the air of the hall.

The moment his voice poured forth the marble dancers started. Innumerable forms of beauty stepped down and crowded the dance floor. One with his music, the quick interweaving crowd glided along the interlocking mosaics.

Oda stared in speechless astonished admiration. As Finnian sang, the song filled him completely as long as he thought of the Beech—

Show me now the world in truth ...

He began . . . but then what flowed through him became the language of the trees and he felt himself altered in spirit with a rush of inexpressible joy. The music continued as did the dancers but Finnian hardly noticed any movement outside his own soul. The exultant strains were sustained for mere minutes, no more. The singer began to fear his own influence. Finnian felt unable to bear up under the weight of beauty, his mind cast about and notes merged into a great cacophony. The music shuddered, wavered, and then came to a halt. Each figure sprang back to its pedestal and stood rigid. Silence rolled in like thunder. The song had ceased.

Finnian leaned against Oda and wept exhausted with joy. Oda sat blubbering beside him.

Both wished it could have lasted longer. Both were relieved it was over.

"Where did you learn to sing?" asked Oda.

Looking into the austere face of Oda, Finnian still felt guarded. In spite of the heights of just-shared experience he was reticent. Her nature possessed little empathetic gentleness. She carried the pain of Ciara close and it touched her every word with him. But . . . here they sat, she the only one who had seen what the music had done. Here they sat, the only animated two in all of the ten marble halls. Here they sat, sharing tears over the unexplainable.

14

Five Words

O DA TOUCHED HIS ARM and asked again, "Where did you learn to sing?"

Finnian cast about in his mind for a place to begin. The Beech? No, to tell of the Beech was to tell of the Ash, and to tell of the Ash touched on the Alder. Oda, after all, had been the first to warn him to distinguish between the trees. He started instead with the marble cave.

He began his tale when he found shelter in the cave from the beating sun and ended when the lady disappeared into the wood. He told of the soft cool moss and the wonder of the intricate bas-relief. He spoke of the smooth artistry of marble inlaid in alabaster. He pointed to where the patterns lay all about them in the hall, etched into every pedestal. He told of the song that had come over him, speaking the lyrics to Oda, careful not to add the tune. He told Oda of the lady's beauty and how she rushed away. He told all he intended and no more, not one hint of trunk nor branch of Alder or Ash. But though Finnian remained within his self-made boundaries, he inadvertently displayed his tender underbelly. Oda knew without doubt that before her sat a man smitten with a beauty beyond his reach.

She allowed him to ramble uninterrupted, nodding and enrapt at the place in the story where the music made impact. When Finnian finished Oda took a deep breath. She turned to her companion laying a hand on his shoulder and said, "I have heard of the marble lady." Then she looked straight into Finnian's forlorn eyes and shattered him with five words, "She belongs to another man."

Her words demolished all sense of the bond so recently established between them. Finnian did not question the word's veracity. Oda's truthfulness was beyond question. He simply could not take the words in. Her statement hit with a great thud against his chest and for a moment, he could not breathe.

Finnian recoiled and scowled. Distressed and disoriented, he nearly spoke his thoughts aloud: . . . but I woke her . . . am I not to be given a chance? Does she not know it was I? The Beech tree wanted me and wept when I departed. Why should the marble lady give me no consideration at all?

Oda saw him struggle within himself and said with earnest sincerity, "Finnian, I hope you know I am a friend who has no wish to shake apart your dream."

"My hopes and dreams are none of your affair, Lady Oda," said Finnian, chafed. He rose as if to go.

Oda stifled a rising wave of frustrated pity. What of the hopes and dreams of my cousin Ciara? she thought, but replied in long-disciplined dispassion, "Of course you want a pretty girl to travel beside you through life. Every man I've ever met wants the same. It is not hard to guess at your hopes and dreams."

"You do not know me," hissed Finnian. "You have no right . . ."

She caught his hand. "You move in visions, Finnian; I move in the grittiness of life. Forgive me for my frankness." Her voice softened even more, "And thank you for your singing tonight. The dance was wonderful. More than I could have ever expected. You brought comfort to me in ways you do not know."

Finnian loosed his hand but waited as she rose to walk beside him.

They traveled in complete silence until reaching the corridor which turned towards Oda's room. She stopped and gazed at her companion in the dim candlelight flickering along the hallway. "Do not give in to loneliness and vain thoughts, dear Finnian. They are the nets of your dogged shadow."

His face blackened.

She tried again, "You are not alone. I am here, not your first choice, I realize, but it is something. And, there is much more to the statues than we yet know. We will find out together."

Finnian could not hear. As he left her, his heart rolled around in his chest, a rough stone newly chipped from the quarry. Who was she to mention his shadow? What did she know of him? Didn't everyone have one, herself included? Shadows came and went. In a land like this, with so many illusions everywhere, his shadow had been helpful in disenchanting his childish fancies. She had said herself that he moved too much in visions.

Well, Finnian said to himself, disdaining the tenderness of his own heart, let my shadow be the cure. True, it would have been best if I had never opened that cursed door—never given him so much ground. But good is worked from missteps. It is the way of the Universe.

Simmering in such thoughts, Finnian put himself to bed and fell into erratic slumber.

He awoke midmorning, numbed and hardened, determined to play the fool no more, to fall for vanities no longer. I will not see beauty and wonder where there is none, he told himself, I will dare to behold things as they are. He let his feet fall upon the thick carpet and stretched himself to full height. Relaxing he glanced down and saw a note had been slipped under his door. It was an invitation to breakfast with Oda in the kitchen.

He decided not to go and haughtily mulled over the idea that she was sweet on him. Yes, that was the root of their trouble. After all, Oda was quite plain compared to her cousin. Women grew bitter with envy over such inequalities.

Finnian went directly to the sunroom fountain. Lost in thought he did not hear the tramp of a great horse ringing through the gateway, the clang of armor in the courtyard, the thud of a rider dismounting. Nor did he note the rider's gentle words to his companion as she alighted on the pavement next to him.

15

A Couple at the Fountain

FINNIAN STRIPPED OFF HIS WELL-TAILORED CLOTHES, tossing them aside into the alcove. There was no tenderness in his hands for the once beloved gift. He thought no more about his suit than he did the untidied room and unmade bed he left behind that morning. Most irritating, though the fact boiled below conscious thought, was that he had grown used to breakfast being delivered. The palace was losing its enchantment.

Diving into the escape of the sea, he wondered what place of solitude might next be invaded by the other resident of the palace. He would not tell Oda of the fountain-portal to the wondrous expanse. She could find it on her own.

He exerted himself swimming in his anger, several times coming up for breath. The third time his lips and nostrils broke the surface, he found he was not alone. He froze in the water, careful to remain hidden below the lip of the marble bowl. He heard hushed voices speaking. The dim shadow of a delicate lady nestled in the arms of a tall muscular lover flickered against the dome.

"O my beloved, you are safe and we have arrived home. I am blessed."

Her soft fingers were speedily overcoming all the remaining clasps of his armor. One by one she undid the lacings of his boots. When both stood unclothed ready for the healing waters, the lady again sprang into well-built arms and laid her head where she could feel the beating of his heart.

All this Finnian saw in shadows. His presence remained unknown. He thought to wait until they were about to enter, take in one large breath, and dive beneath. He would conceal himself behind nearby coral until the couple swam out to sea. Until then, he was trapped as a witness to intimacies meant for two not three. He leaned in, listening for coming footsteps across the tile.

The lady had disengaged herself from her man's embrace and moved about to care for his belongings, folding and stacking them neatly in an alcove opposite where Finnian had hastily discarded his own. The man stood, a mighty form crowned with a noble head, watching her move with purpose. Finnian supposed his face glowed with love.

And then Finnian realized he knew him. It was Sir Dunstan. And, given Dunstan's character, the lady could only be his bride. Finnian's stomach grew queasy as he realized he was privy to the secrets of a friend.

The lady led her husband to a bench near the fountain and sat on a grassy mat near his feet. The tiles were warm for the room was well heated. This delay left Finnian torn. He was loathe to hear more but glad he was not holding his breath behind coral wondering whether or not he could go up again. He could not imagine a dignified way to add a third naked body to the atmosphere of intimacy. If only the room were not so perfectly heated! Then she would not sit and prattle on and on. The couple would dive beneath the warmness of the waves.

"You seem distracted, Dunstan," she began.

"While I am glad, my darling, that we are well and reunited," her husband answered, "I can't forget our friend, met twice in the forest. There was something noble in him, but it was a nobility of thought and not of deed. He may yet perish from vile fear. It troubles me sometimes."

"You saved him, darling, from Ash and Alder. And since a man cannot save another from his own fear, nothing more can be asked of you."

"And he saved *you*, Lenora, and for that he will never leave my mind until I know he is out of danger."

Finnian's heart nearly stopped. There was no one he had saved, save one.

Dunstan continued, "You tell me he roused you with a song from the death-sleep of an evil enchantment and now I fear he is fallen under one himself."

"And you rescued him so he had the chance to fight on," interposed Lenora. "You struck your battle-axe again and again into the Ash. A lesser man would not do so much for one he had already warned."

Sir Dunstan sighed, remembering the battle. Endurance had conquered in the end for there are horrors that force alone cannot overcome. Finnian shuddered as he treaded water. The couple in the sunroom sat in their nakedness, stripping him bare. Trapped and helpless he was torn to pieces by two he loved.

"My heart feels bound to him, and I wish to protect him, but I think, dear wife, that you may love him somewhat."

At these words Finnian trembled. He no longer chose to go or to stay. He listened now with great intent.

"Ah!" she replied. "How can I help it? By his love he woke me from worse than death. I would never have found you again, if he had not sought me first."

"You are right," returned her husband. "It would be impossible not to return his love for the kind of gift he gave you. I, too, am indebted to him, more than words can speak."

Lenora's silhouette flickered on the ceiling as she rose. She stood apart from Dunstan and now addressed him with firm authority, "I love Finnian but not as I love you.

He was the moon of my night. You are the sun of my day, O beloved."

Sir Dunstan arose. The conversation was over. Hand in hand they moved towards the fountain. One at a time they disappeared below the waves. Finnian trembled behind the coral and let them swim silently past.

Out and undetected, he dressed as an ocean of sighs froze in his bosom. He could remain no longer. She who his soul sought had entered his abode. Or more accurately, he seemed to have entered hers. Either way, to remain at the palace would mean to see her daily and in the arms of one loved better than he. This he could not bear.

16

A Pit of Shame and Shadow

INNIAN DID NOT RETURN TO HIS ROOM. He would be long gone before the swimmers sought him out. The linchpin to his imagined world of heroism had been removed. The lady of the marble was real flesh and blood, no longer a central figure of internal fantasy. She had a name: Lady Lenora, wife of Sir Dunstan. He was a side character—one to be troubled over, one to be rescued.

He went the way of the kitchen hoping both to see, and not to see, Oda. He found her. She saw at once no language would penetrate the coil of shame-wrapped anger. She knew he was leaving from his steady silence. As he paced, she packed him a bag of provisions that would travel well. She knew his tastes. He did not notice.

Away Finnian wandered to find the farthest exit from the grand front entrance and the river that had borne him to his haven. Through back corridors unexplored he tramped, feeling nothing as he left, noticing nothing as he passed familiar sights and sounds. At last he saw a pale yellow lamp hanging above a heavy, rough door, altogether unlike any other portal in the palace. It was neither ebony inlaid with ivory, nor ivory inlaid with silver. It had none of the ornate woodwork and beauty Finnian had begun to take for granted. Old oak with heavy nails and iron studs blocked his way.

It took all his effort to push it open.

Stepping through, he leaned into a windy corridor. A cold gust came head-on. Massive rocks like tombstones stood in all directions. A roof, supported by iron beams, covered a wall-less walkway in front of him stretching for miles. Finnian walked every step of those miles, hour after lonely hour, not caring or counting. When the path ended he saw nothing but a great hole in the earth. Steps, chiseled evenly into the ancient rock, invited him down into a cavernous chamber. He did not gaze into the chasm but without pause in his well-paced stride continued down. The opening received him, jaws gaping perpendicular as a large excavated well. The staircase led round and round the gulf, descending spirally into the abyss. He could perceive no bottom.

Finnian welcomed the heartless, tortuous descent into nothingness. He gave no thought to returning to the palace even when the steps gave way to ledges and the ledges to bare toe-holds. He did not second-guess himself even when forced to cling to the rocks like a bat.

Having lost track of the hours but sensing he had descended a long way, Finnian looked up and saw stars. Below him, the shaft went sheer down, smooth as glass. The reflective surface became a twinkling burrow, sides and ceiling projecting a glittering display of constellations. By comparison, the unfolding symmetrical patterns of the palace faded in their man-made artfulness. Here was beauty beyond telling. Here he could drown in self-forgetting wonder. He thought for a moment of free-falling. But his legs reengaged in their step upon rhythmic step.

In less than ten yards he encountered a narrow opening. Leaving behind the mesmerizing night sky, he entered. Once through the passage broadened. The sky became rock. Stalactites and stalagmites formed new paths branching off on every side. In-between passageways opened up into great halls before him and closed just as suddenly behind. He found himself wandering an underground labyrinth as his path went ever downwards. His ash-grey thoughts grew darker, and all idea of ever returning to the sunlit surface dissipated into forgetfulness.

Only when his food ran out was he nudged by unmet need. Stomach gurgling, he awakened into dread. The region he had wandered into was not uninhabited. He was surrounded by the unknown presence of many.

Finnian had heard of trolls before but had not given them much thought. What little notions he had formed made him think they were bigger and lumbered about alone. He had no idea the subterranean creatures might infest in packs. Clusters of them ran elbow-nudging and babbling back and forth across his path like adolescents. In and out they wove in front of his slow trudge, pausing to consult among themselves with exaggerated gestures. Undiluted mocking peals of laughter rang forth against the cavern walls.

The roving gangs gathered as one and began to sing. The lyrics were nonsense but the tone was that of mock entreaty and worship. A loud-mouthed leader would create a verse and the rest would echo back in chorus growing louder and more robust with each repetition. Then the horde would shout with laughter, roaring and dancing and flinging themselves on the ground in pretended convulsions of delight. Finnian had no doubt that he was the butt of some great joke. With the feeling came the fear that they somehow knew a great deal about him. His dismay and shame were public here and in the hands of trolls.

The loudest and longest solo reached a crescendo and the chorus of backup singers ringed round their unwitting audience of one. The maestro climbed atop a high stalagmite and, turning heels over head several times in his descent, landed feet first on Finnian's shoulders. There he swayed with extraordinary balance for so ungainly a creature, somehow keeping both himself and his host upright. Finnian thought he would soon crumble under the weight of the narcissistic parasite, as the towering troll gyrated and wagged his tongue. He made grotesque

*Undiluted mocking peals of laughter rang against
the cavern walls.*

gesticulations with his pelvis and hindquarters, egged on by the cries and jeers of his eager audience. Then came a shower of stones from innumerable hands.

The rocks cut Finnian's arms and face as the troll atop him sprang free of the projectiles. Finnian attempted to run, but the mob all rushed upon him, laying hold of every part that could be grasped, holding him tight. Swarming like yellow jackets in his face and ears they shouted abuse and invectives, chanting—

> *You shan't have her! You shan't have her!*
> *She is for a better man,*
> *Better man, better man.*
> *How he kisses her! How he kisses her!*
> *Better man, better man*
> *Bet – her – man*

The torrent of battery went on and on. Tears of mortifying terror streamed down Finnian's cheeks, tears he could not reach and wipe away. His clothes ripped under the claws and teeth. The nakedness of body began to match the nakedness of soul.

Salvation came in the smallest of pauses. The horde stopped for a split second, taking a collective breath. In that small space, as the trolls girded themselves for a second round to the death, Finnian said aloud, "He is a better man. He should have her."

The two simple phrases struck the trolls like much-feared sunshine. They dropped their prey and fell back a step or two with a whole broadside of grunts and humphs. They kicked at the dust of their cavern playground, all at once confused as to their purpose.

Finnian pulled himself to his feet. Tattered and bloodied, he made a wobbly step forward. A lane was instantly opened for him. He walked a few yards and looked back to see them all standing still, looking after him, like a great squad of reprimanded school boys.

Finnian, like a second act of a marvelous opera, replaced their hateful singing with his own—

I will weep aside;
It is well that you should be,
My nobler brother's bride.
Let me then be thy moon of night
And he be as thy day
Waxing waning hid from sight
Bring comfort as I may

All fell silent as Finnian went on his way.

17

A Vessel Upon the Ocean

PULLED FROM HIS NUMBNESS, spared by the trolls—though he hardly understood how—Finnian trudged on, hungry and half-naked. His heart oscillated moment-to-moment between despondency and the conviction that he should return to the palace and submit himself to the wisdom of Oda. The trolls' delight in drawing blood, their accurate slashing candor, had revealed what he could not before take in. Oda's honest speech was the faithful wounding of a friend. Her cutting kindness had been love, and that of the highest caliber.

He recoiled, looking back. His pain-induced selfishness had not even asked after her mother. How came she to abide alone, tending him secretly from the lowliness of the palace kitchen? And what of his suit of clothes? Had she sewn them as well? All that remained now of the coat were the cuffs, dangling from his wrists.

The pain that sent Finnian down into the pit no longer held his heart. The love between Dunstan and Lenora no longer strangled him. A song had called a beautiful woman back to life and he had played a part—that was all.

An unspeakable tenderness for her remained, but passionate desire had been brought to heel.

Yet, while the conviction grew that he should return to the company of proven friends, obedience to new-found wisdom remained impossible. Finnian had no idea which direction the palace lay. The underground labyrinth had not grown more discernible just because trolls now stayed out of his way.

A hard right turn lay ahead and Finnian found himself in a gallery of stalactites so warped and bulging that from below they look like massive cocoons ready to burst. The rocky structures crowded ever downward from above, the ceiling lowering with his every step. The stalagmites grew up from the floor, both on the left hand and the right, crowded in as well. In his hunkered march, he could now reach and touch both side walls with outstretched hands. The roof sank ever lower. The walls squeezed in. He became compelled first to stoop, and then to creep on his hands and knees.

At last, moving himself along on his belly through the ever-narrowing passage, a pinhole of long-forgotten daylight shone ahead. The shard of sunshine compelled Finnian to overcome the last short distance to escape the tunnel into the sun that shone on the unknown next.

Finnian found himself upon the shore of a wintry sea. The sun hung just a few feet above the horizon. A grey beach of loose stones stretched miles and miles in both directions. Hundreds of hopeless waves rushed shoreward. There was nothing for the eye but mingling shades of colorlessness and nothing for the ear but the break and roar of retreating wave. The moan of a cold, death-like wind swept across the shore from the pale mouth of clouds upon the horizon. Signs of life were nowhere. The foam rushed higher up the stones and a few dead stars began to gleam in the east.

A sandbar along a low platform of rock ran far out into the midst of the breaking waters and along it Finnian now scrambled. Over the smooth stones he hastened towards the tumbling chaos, not always keeping his feet against the wind and sea. When he reached the end of the low promontory the fall and rise of the waves pounded against him with their spray.

He wondered if other pilgrims made to endure bellycrawling humiliation emerged into a world of grey meaninglessness, no better off than before entering the crucible. He stared at the sea feeling unchanged beyond the crippling weight of regret, exhaustion, and that damned shadow that continued to cling to the tattered remains of his front pocket.

"I will not be tortured to death," Finnian cried. "I will meet it halfway." And with these words he plunged headlong into the mounting waves below. A blessing, like the kiss of a mother, alit on his soul bringing with it a calm, deeper than the fathoms beneath him. He sank far into the waters and did not seek to return.

But the ocean would not let him drown. He was lifted with loving arms to the surface to take in breath again. But his eyes remained tight shut, refusing to look on the wintry sea and the pitiless low-hanging sky.

This was the same wide sea Finnian had so often entered through the palace fountain. And as he floated listless in the water, a little vessel was brought alongside by those he had swum with unaware, day after day. They had perceived his exploits, fleshed-out and fantastical; his falls from grace, real and imagined; the beauty of his weaknesses and his damaging strengths. The little multi-colored hull rose and sank on the waters, nudging him gently as it fell. It glistened against the greyness of the ocean and sky, covered in scales of brilliant hues. Finnian half climbed, half rolled aboard. Laying down in the hull, he drew over himself a heavy purple cloth and fell asleep, overcome with fatigue.

The boat—seatless, oarless, provisionless—was no more than a floating cradle, moving upon the ever-quickening current, its rider senseless to time and space. Dreams of unspeakable joy came upon him—of restored friendships, of revived embraces, of love which said it had never died, of faces that had vanished long ago. He dreamt of pardons implored and granted with such bursting floods of love that he was almost glad he had sinned.

When Finnian awoke, the boat was floating motionless by the grassy shore of a little island.

18

Green Eyes in a Grass Hut

THE WATER WAS FATHOMS DEEP right up to where it kissed the edge of the island shore. Finnian stumbled from the little boat upon a soft grassy turf covered in varying grasses and tiny flowers. Delicate lowly things were most plentiful, but no trees nor hill nor rock rose skywards.

The whole island lay open to the sky. Far out ocean waves tossed no more than a few feet above the level sea. Along the shore, deep, clear, unrippled waters rose and fell pulse-like. Neither tide nor storm seemed to have touched the isle.

Standing in the calm, persistent fullness, Finnian turned to bid his vessel goodbye. It was now a dim speck floating out towards the horizon.

Finnian turned back again. As if it had grown up from the very soil itself, a square hut now stood in the center of the island. Low walls covered in thatch bore up a high pyramidal roof of long reeds. Withered blossoms hung over all the eaves. It had no windows but a single door in the center of each side. Finnian strolled towards it over the pathless grass, blade and stem springing up again as the weight of his footfalls lifted.

Finnian knocked on the partly open door and the sweetest voice he had ever heard said, "Come in." A bright fire was burning on a hearth centered in the clay floor. There was no chimney and smoke found its way up and out through an opening in the center of the reedy roof. Over the fire hung a little pot, and over the pot bent a woman.

The oldest and most wonderful countenance Finnian had ever beheld looked up and smiled. There was not a spot in which a wrinkle could lie, where a wrinkle lay not. Her skin was ancient and brown like old parchment. Her form was tall and spare and when she stood, she stood straight as an arrow. Though her wrinkled eyelids were old, and heavy, and worn, her eyes were absolutely young. They belonged to a woman of five-and-twenty—large and clear, they shone green incarnations of soft light. She held out her hand to him and gave greeting with a single word, "Welcome."

Finnian kissed her hand and took up an old wooden chair near the fire. She bent back over to continue her cooking like a mother whose boy had just arrived home, having crossed miles of hills through heavy storms of wind and snow. She brought out from the little pot some of the dish she had prepared, and set two bowls on a linen-covered table beside him. They ate in silence.

Afterward, Finnian took both of her wrinkled hands in his and burst into happy tears. She put a gentle arm round him saying, "Though I did not expect you quite so soon, I am glad that you are here."

THE TWO PULLED THEIR CHAIRS UP beside the gentle flames, and the woman drew to herself a lute. She began to sing. An amazing store of poetry cascaded from her lips over river stones of ancient tunes. As she sang, she wept gently and plentifully. The heartfelt tears did not cause a waver in the melody nor a warble in the rhythm. Tears, it seemed to Finnian, fell for both everyone she had ever loved and just for him alone. Music melded seamlessly with sorrow.

With a gentle sigh just escaping, a second set of melodies began. Born in her heart, they shook her whole frame. Underneath the tune hovered cries of fear and suppressed pain. The final chorus was a low moan. Her neck remained unbent, her head held aloft throughout, her eyes ever open, though her face grew white as death. At length the woman glanced towards Finnian, like a mother who checks to see whether her child is well. During the second set of songs, her guest had fallen asleep.

As he slept under the sheltering arc of her music, Finnian dreamt of the womanly Beech, lovely and solemn; the beauty of Lenora, gliding through the sunlit beams;

the shattered innocence of Ciara; and the quiet determination of Oda. He awoke half-aware that his hostess had been singing all the strands of his meandering story, intermingling them as one.

The woman smiled when she saw that his eyes were open.

"You sing beautifully," he effused half-awake, caught up in reverie.

"As do you," she replied softly.

Finnian answered her, only halfway and only in his head: I have not sung a single note in your hut and somehow you know. Then aloud, "Only as the music comes upon me. The songs are my masters, not I theirs."

"Do you think it is any different for me?" she returned.

"Yes, I do, my lady. I think the songs come from *within* you."

His hostess did not argue but Finnian saw a smile despite her tears. The smile upon the withered face with young eyes filled her countenance and radiated light.

She rose. With a warm cloth she bathed his face and hands and put more food before him. As he ate she pulled out a coat and tunic from an ancient chest in the corner. Neither were as fine and bright as what Oda had created, but Finnian knew somehow that the garments had been waiting there for him to come, ages on end.

III

Finnian said, "The fight is long and hard and I fear that I will never conquer myself much less my shadow."

"You have not actually fought for life and death as yet," she returned. "And corrosive shadows must be slain before dragons and giants. Otherwise something worse may come upon you."

"I fear too much. And I am deeply ashamed of my constant tears."

The old woman smiled. "Present tears are future strength," said she, "and tears are the only cure for weeping."

When Finnian wiped his mouth at last, she looked at him and said, "Listen to me, my child. You cannot stay here."

"Leave!" Finnian cried out alarmed, "I am so happy with you. I never was so happy in all my life."

"But you must go," she said with sadness in her voice. "Listen! What do you hear?"

Finnian cocked his head and replied, "I hear the sound of a great surging of many waters."

"The waters around this cottage will rise and flow and come, till they form a firmament over this dwelling. As long as I keep my fire burning the water cannot enter, but neither can any leave. What you must do must be done outside these walls. There is not much time for your escape."

"But how can I go if the waters are all about?"

"The doors in this cottage lead out, but not always to where you expect. I will show you through the right one."

She kissed him and bade him goodbye with a solemnity and ceremony that awed and bewildered him.

With some trepidation in her voice she said, "You will come back to me someday, I know. But I beg you, for my sake, to remember one thing. In whatever sorrow you find yourself, however inconsolable and irremediable it may appear, believe that the old woman in the grass hut with the green eyes knows something, though she cannot tell it in a way that would satisfy your understanding. In the worst moments of your distress, remember she knows and loves. Now go, my son, and do something worth doing."

Finnian kissed her cheek and felt as if he were leaving his mother for the first time.

She took his hand and led him out into the open air. Unable to bear looking again into her clear green eyes, he took strength in the echo of her singing that trailed after him—

> *Better to sit at the waters' birth,*
> *Than a sea of waves to win*
> *To live in the love that floweth forth,*
> *Than the love that cometh in.*
> *We weep for gladness, weep for grief*
> *The tears they are the same*

The Forging of Finnian Ludwell

We sigh for longing, and relief
The sighs have but one name,
The pangs of death are throbs of life,
Each are both the same

19

Brothers at the Forge

F INNIAN FOUND HIMSELF STANDING AGAIN in the deep grassy turf. The soft sponge under his feet brought back his initial steps onto the island from the mer-boat. The little vessel that had sustained him had been taken back out to sea by its makers. There was no leaving by the way he had come.

Hearing the click of the door a few feet behind, he turned to bid the grass hut, where he had just sung and supped, farewell. It was a dim speck on a far horizon. With one step he now stood alone on an open plain. It was no longer an island but a wind-blown isthmus. The water was rising, the sod soaked with the tide, and scrambling was necessary to make it to higher rockier ground. On each side of Finnian the sea rose rapidly—but without wind, or violent motion, or broken waves.

He hurried his pace not just for the sake of life and limb, but because to hold still was to drown in an ocean of thought. He was being sent back to face his agony, to serve those he had loved, whom he now loved more truly.

A mile in from the sea he reached open, rough country, proceeding in as straight a line as the terrain would allow. The sun was high and attempting with all its might to break through the grey. Coming over a crest of seaward rock, the landscape changed to golden and green. Pines dotted the countryside and in their midst stood a lonely stone tower. It seemed the same leaning tower he had spied through the library window.

The outpost, built on the top of a little hill overlooking the neighboring kingdoms, was larger than he had imagined. It loomed now before him, a stone's throw away, no longer a distant prop for his copious fantasies. Erect among the pines the tower sat on ancient foundations, formidable in spite of fissuring fault lines that crawled through the century-old masonry.

As Finnian approached, he heard the clang of an anvil. Rapid came the blows, then a pause, and then renewed efforts of vigorous pounding. He knocked loudly. The door was pulled open by a noble-looking youth, half-undressed, glowing with heat. He was begrimed with the blackness of the forge and in one hand held a sword that shone with a dull fire. The smell of earth and flame together wafted out to dissipate among the needled branches. The youth studied Finnian's face and cracked a wide grin. The door was thrown open wide and with a low bow the guest was invited in. Finnian found himself inside a rustic hall-turned-forge that occupied the whole of the ground floor.

*In one hand he held a sword that shone with a
dull fire*

A huge fire roared in the massive hearth. Beside the anvil, in similar undress and with hammer in hand, stood Sir Dunstan. In a glance Finnian knew the two were brothers.

WHILE DUNSTAN WAS MUSCULAR AND DARK, with curling hair and large hazel eyes that sometimes grew wondrously soft, his brother was slender and fair. His countenance reminded Finnian of an eagle, brown eyes shining with an almost fierce expression. He stood erect, as if looking from a lofty mountain crag over a vast plain outstretched below.

Dunstan smiled and spoke, "Welcome, Finnian, will you sit and rest, till we finish this part of our work?"

Finnian sat. Dunstan thrust the sword in the fire, brought it to sufficient heat, drew it out, and laid it on the anvil. There his brother, with a succession of quick smart blows, hammered it straight and sharp. Finally it was plunged into a vessel full of waiting water. Blue flame sprang upwards as the glowing steel entered.

The brothers left the blade to rest and drew up two stools facing Finnian.

Dunstan began, "We have been hoping for your return for some days. Brendan and I," and here Brendan offered a sooty hand which Finnian clasped gladly, "need your aid."

"How might *I* be useful?" replied Finnian, overwhelmed that these two warriors should be looking for, much less joyous at his coming. He looked about the forge. "I have little skill in metal craft, and as you seem to be readying yourselves for battle, I must confess to *no* combat experience."

Both brothers nodded in vigorous agreement during Finnian's confession of his un-usefulness. But both seemed anxious that their guest not leave. Finnian could make no sense it.

"Swordsmanship and metallurgy can be taught. We need a third man. We need *you* as that third," said Brendan.

Finnian furrowed his brow and crossed his arms, unsure of his inclusion. He was uncertain if Dunstan remembered anything of him at all from their short travels together.

"Oda has told us of your songs among the statues," Dunstan clarified.

"Will you sing for our side?" followed up Brendan softly.

Finnian sat as one mute—overwhelmed at being wanted and convinced he would disappoint. Yes, he sang, but he could neither begin nor sustain the music. The songs came upon him as they wished. Additionally, while he had survived the onslaught of more than one foe since coming to Capgrave, dumb luck and the kindness of others had rescued him. It had nothing to do, by any stretch of the imagination, with his own courage.

The confident pursuit of Brendan and Dunstan was bewildering.

Both brothers took Finnian's silence as a show of ignorance rather than cowardice. Both rushed to fill in the missing details.

"Ah! He does not know about it," said Brendan. "You must tell him, Dunstan, from the first."

Dunstan looked at Finnian's blank face and nodded. "Our father is king of this country. You, when you are not off exploring the surrounding seas, and I, Oda, and . . . my wife . . . have all come under the same roof in the king's summer palace at Biscop. Brendan here rode up yesterday bringing news that a long-brewing crisis has come to a head."

Brendan rose and filled three goblets and put one into each man's hand. He settled in again to hear his brother tell the tale.

Dunstan began, "Seven years ago, three giant brothers appeared on the outskirts of our kingdom, just west of Capgrave."

Finnian nodded, recalling the home of Oda and Aelryth.

"The giants took possession of a ruined castle on the westernmost edge of the realm: Wittan Towers. The towers had stood unchanged as far back as any of the local country people remember. Repairing has never been a priority for our father, being greatly distracted by other matters.

"Because the giants were rarely seen, and at first caused no mischief, they were regarded by Wittan's neighbors as harmless, perhaps even benevolent. Old Wittan castle had breaches in the lower part of the walls and the giants built them up. Then they repaired battlements. Folks in the area allayed their nagging fears by telling themselves that the repairs would prevent the historical site from falling into worse decay while the interior was being restored.

"Then one brave villager concealed himself and, in an all-night vigil, watched the giants work. The next morning he reported to the town council that the three uninvited residents worked with all their energy to restore the massive stones of the grand turnpike stair in the citadel. He revealed as well that the giants had connected the round tower to the ramparts, which had been completed stealthily foot-by-foot over the previous year.

"The concerned council documented all the activity in an official report which all members signed and had notarized. The town scribe wrote reports in triplicate and the original was sealed and placed in the town lock box. But the magistrate could find no legal pretext for interfering and no one suggested the real reason for letting the giants alone—fear.

"Two weeks later not a breach in the walls remained, and citizens could hear the clanging anvil on what must be the reforging of the great iron gates. But the giants, though they had no deed to the castle, lived in peace with all. Those who called for action were now accused of fear-mongering.

"It was found, in hindsight, that the three giants had distant kin among the town folks and family ties were respected. But when these relatives grew old and died, the giants proceeded to spoil the countryside. Houses around the rebuilt castle were pillaged. The giants began to make themselves fat off the labor of others, feasting sumptuously within the walls of Wittan."

Dunstan took a long drink from his goblet and then turned to Brendan. "Bren," he said, "You should take the tale from here since you saw much of it firsthand."

Brendan did not answer. For while Finnian was captivated by Dunstan's every word, Brendan had been staring into the fire, his heart miles away on another topic altogether.

20

Doubts and Distractions

DUNSTAN KICKED THE WOODBLOCK-TURNED-FOOTSTOOL out from beneath his little brother's feet and Brendan came back to present location and company with a thud. "I was just saying, dear brother," said Dunstan laughing, "that you should take the tale from here, being a firsthand witness."

"Were we talking giants or dragons?" Brendan asked with a sleepy wink. "You really should enliven your skills as a storyteller."

Prompted on where to begin, Brendan picked up where Dunstan left off, "News of the giants' robberies came to our father's ears but he has lately been crippled in his resources by a protracted war with a neighboring prince. (It's a long royal family squabble, Finnian, I will spare you.) He could send only a very few soldiers to attempt the capture of Wittan. The giants slew every man.

"The slaying of knights caused the titans to grow bolder. Feeling no consequences for their crimes, they no longer confined their plundering to property and began to seize persons. Common folk, knights, and ladies have suffered all manner of indignities. The giants were partial, still are I'm afraid, to putting citizens to torture until they are redeemed for exorbitant ransoms. Many warriors have gone out to fight them on their own without our father's orders, but all so far have been overthrown, slain, or captured. To stamp out all attempts at their overthrow, the giants now put one or more of their captives to a shameful death if any man attempts to breech the walls of Wittan.

"No one has made an attempt to storm the towers for nearly a year now for dread of seeing more heads left on turrets in sight of all passers-by."

Brendan paused to let the story sink in. He threw his cup down and it shattered against the stones, stood, and continued with a voice low and vehement, "It is the responsibility of the king and his sons to defend our citizens. Since Dunstan and I learned the extent of the ongoing tragedy we have carried a fiery burden to attack these demons and destroy them."

Brendan stepped to the fire and poked about in the glowing embers, turned and looked Finnian full in the face, "It is because of current captives we have not dared. But we ponder the quest continually. Now that we know of your gifts and abilities, Finnian, we are emboldened. The statues move again."

Brendan fell quiet and Dunstan completed the brothers' appeal, "Two princes are no match for three giants but . . .

we know beyond doubt you are sent to us and belong with us."

Finnian's heart was filled with loving admiration. He stood and threw off his upper garments and said, "I am ashamed of my white tender hands when yours are so nobly soiled and hard. Put me to work and may all that shames your noble family soon be wiped away."

"No, no!" Dunstan cried smiling, "We will work no more today. Rest is as needful as toil. Bring the supper, Brendan. It is your evening to serve."

The younger brother brought to the table dried meat, nuts, and fruits. Good wine made up for the fare. The three ate and drank heartily, raising a toast to present song and future deeds. Both Dunstan and Brendan had been pondering the coming conflict for some time. Each had reason to believe he would perish—perish victoriously, but perish. Each thought Finnian was the harbinger of a success that would outlive them both.

Dunstan dreaded his coming death because of his love for Lenora. Having achieved the highest possible happiness, his bride being a greater gift than he could possibly deserve, his poet's heart was sure life had peaked and he would now die in the height of his prime.

Brendan's reasons for dread were more complex. He feared his brother and he would leave their father, the old king, childless. Though the king was loved by both sons, Brendan ministered to the infirmities of growing age, listening with patience to the old man's tales of youthful adventures. Brendan had not lost in the smallest degree the conviction that his father was the most noble man in the world. He longed to return to him laden with the spoils of the hated giants. And, besides his love for his father, Brendan's mind had begun of late to be occupied by a young lady newly residing at Biscop. This second dread he hid, even from himself.

Both Dunstan and Brendan feared that when the moment of decision came in the heat of battle, each might be distracted by love for others. Both wanted to give themselves fully over to the ideal of death with honor—to die for the freedom of all souls in the kingdom. They wanted the well-honed weapon of a singular goal.

The three men dined until the sun was long sunk over the horizon leaving the tower room lit only by torches. Dunstan expressed only briefly his fears of leaving a widow, knowing Finnian's past heroics and current tenderness towards his wife. Brendan spoke of his love of father with complete transparency. But both of his listeners, especially Dunstan, suspected a second distraction.

For his own part, Finnian did not dread death. He had no one he cared for more than the two men with whom he supped. He dreaded the encounter with the giants because of the responsibility connected with the battle, but he resolved to grow cool, and quick, and forceful. He had also learned, in the course of the evening's conversations, that both Oda's father and mother were among the captives within Wittan's dark towers.

21

A Song for One, A Meeting of Two

FINNIAN AWOKE LONG BEFORE THE BROTHERS in the morning. He hoped to slip away and return without either noting his absence, and wondered how the great door, impossible to close without a heavy thud, did not wake anyone.

Their confidence in his singing needed to be tested alone. If he succeeded, he would give himself over to their idea of a band of three. If he failed, he must leave Biscop and find a way to exit Capgrave altogether. He would savor their night of song like love that was not meant to be. It had been beautiful fun to play along, but what had he to do with nobility? He, who slipped in and out of shadow worlds through words on a page, belonged to no one.

With soft quick steps he moved away along the well-cut forest path and then made his way through several acres of royal orchards. On the edge of the final garden stood the same stately Biscop residence that had welcomed him into its mysterious ghostly halls weeks before. Both man and locale had been altered. Whether the difference was his perception of Biscop Palace, the ongoing transformation of himself, or both—Finnian could not tell.

But he did not ruminate within to pinpoint why. He was wholly consumed by his errand.

The dawn had not yet woken the few residents within and Finnian stole up to and through a little-known side entrance on a wing adjacent to the place of his last sorrowful parting. His goal was the marble hall of statuary. He hoped a song would arise within him and awaken just the right sort of assistance.

During the musical interlude shared with Oda, both he and she had noted a muscular man of marble who had *not* stepped down from his pedestal. The colossus had hummed and his toes had tapped, but he had not joined the dance. His reticence was what Finnian remembered and now sought behind the silken curtains.

He made his way stealthily through the hallways, arousing no one. The motionless marble figures were the first human forms to greet him, and in the third ballroom he explored, the chiseled muscular god-of-toe-tapping was found. Perhaps it was the stillness of the hall, perhaps the rare stillness of Finnian's heart, but straightway, to Finnian's great gladness, a song poured forth—

> *Arrows through a moonless sky*
> *What can the blameless do?*
> *What we create, they deign destroy*
> *The courageous are too few*
> *Foes bend their bows upon the string*
> *To pierce my comrades through*

'Gainst self-devouring hatefulness
What can the righteous do?

And the music had the desired effect. More than the desired effect, for it did not awaken the whole company but only the man chosen. The statue blinked and looked down upon the singer.

"Your help is needed in the armory," Finnian told the newly awakened eyes. Then Finnian hummed and the brawny man stood at attention. Finnian whistled and the marbled muscles saluted. Down he stepped from his pedestal, and marched forth. The well-knit sinewy mass stepped brightly alongside Finnian until the whistling melody was cut short by an approaching familiar face.

A lady was crossing the corridor and coming towards them. As the tune dried up between puckered lips, the statue halted and cast about for a pedestal to return to. None were available so the stack of chiseled vigor settled where he stood, into an awkward statuesque pose, nervous hands in front like a fig leaf.

The young woman's countenance was bright and cheerful. Her smile brought back to him the heroine in his favorite book.[10] Finnian smiled back and gaped. When they were within a few yards of passing she stopped and spread her hands palms up asking, "You do know me . . . how do

---

[10] More precisely, his third favorite book—see Appendix 1.

you *not* know me?" Finnian stood by his marble friend, duplicating the stilted pose.

In a somber tone, but without losing her winsome smile, she answered for him, "Aah, but you hurt me, and that, I suppose, makes it easy for a man to forget."

"You broke my globe," she added softly.

Finnian was a man stunned. The beauty before him, confident and shining, was indeed Ciara.

She stepped forward and closed the gap. Finnian did not move. "And I thank you," Ciara continued. "Perhaps I owe you many thanks." Her eyes glowed.

Finnian, mesmerized, was tongue-tied. How well he remembered the shattering and her agony. But now before him he saw the face of a girl glorified into the countenance of a woman.

"I took all the shards to my mother," Ciara confessed. "She wept."

Finnian winced.

"Then to my father. He roared . . . and then laughed."

Of course he did, thought Finnian, looking down. Light words for his daughter's heavy heart. And her brother is no better. But his train of thoughts stopped short. Who was he, the perpetrator, to judge another man?

Ciara persisted, "I journeyed next to Beech and Oak for comfort. They could not help. Afterward, hearing rumors of healing groves and mystical streams, I criss-crossed the kingdom willing to pay any cost to have my globe restored to me, whole and sound. No one could remake the shattering. All instructed me to bury the shards and be done. When I was at my lowest ebb, the Lady of the Alder came to me with inviting words of comfort. She tempted me terribly to turn my sorrow into a dark power over men. But the Oak had reported to me how Lady Alder tore up your belt of Beech, and I was not taken in."

Finnian listened somber, silent, and unflinching. His full attention, heart and soul, was all he had to offer. It felt to him like chaff.

But to Ciara, Finnian's chaff was longed-for gold. So for him, she included a seldom told addendum to her tale, "The shards of my globe are now imbedded in the Alder," Ciara announced, eyes blazing. "She will not soon forget me nor the lies she wove. May the scars remain forever in her as warning to the next despairing girl who goes to her in need of healing mercies."

Finnian dropped to his knees before Ciara, thanking her, begging her to forgive him.

"Rise, rise," she said. "I have nothing to forgive. I thank you. Because of your folly—better, our folly—I do not need a globe to play music now, for I can sing. I could not sing at all before. Now, like you, my songs deliver."

Now both looked into each other's eyes until tears came. A quick embrace was given and then Finnian turned to go.

She touched his shoulder and in a tone most intimate asked, "You work in the armory now with Brendan?"

"Yes. He has much to teach me."

"Keep him safe, please, Finnian. *Please*."

Finnian nodded.

Ciara turned then and addressed the statue, "Wulfric, there is no need to pretend paralysis with two singers present. Go with this man and bless his work. He is my friend."

22

Marble and Soot

A S LONG AS THE KEY WAS MINOR, Wulfric was willing to stay animated for Finnian's softest hum. A famed swordsmith in his time, he inspired and taught the three men in the forge until the day of their decisive battle.

The brothers were respectable bladesmiths, but now Wulfric imparted to Dunstan, Brendan, and Finnian the skill to make heavy mail, shirts of steel plates, a long rapier, a well-balanced saber, a weighted battle-axe, and a hefty two-handed sword. He worked well when Finnian whistled or hummed. He worked miraculously well when Finnian broke forth in song. The three were delighted to find Wulfric knew not only how to make weaponry but could adroitly demonstrate its skillful use, even to the uninitiated. Finnian in particular found him an able teacher, though he had to sing and learn swordplay simultaneously—

> *My enemy not seen as yet*
> *His blood my blade has still to wet*
> *I feel a brazen boldness o'er me grow*
> *Yes, yes, I know and I confess*

A.J. Prufrock

Brendan installed an ebony pedestal in the tower to welcome Wulfric with his own resting place. While Dunstan, Finnian, and Brendan snatched their hours of rest, laying upon workman's cots, Wulfric refused to lie prone but rested in the exact position Finnian had found him—upright, stately, and flexing ever so subtly. A stranger wandering in might wonder at a beautiful besmudged ivory sculpture adorning a blacksmith's workshop. Such an art piece had no place beside belching bellows and acrid smoke. But a stranger never came. In fact all visitors—friends and family not excepted—were considered a dangerous distraction. Labor and exercise continued in rhythmic single-mindedness. Meals were taken at sunrise and sundown in silence. All lighthearted small talk had dissipated into focused meditation.

THE MORNING ARRIVED when Dunstan, Brendan, and Finnian were determined to make the attempt against the giants—to succeed or perish, perhaps both. They resolved to travel on foot for the fright of horses at the appearance of giants often brought defeat before a battle began. The men rose at daybreak, bathed in cold spring water, and dressed in clean garments. As they readied themselves to set out towards Wittan, Finnian took an old lyre found in the tower attic and sang two ballads. The lyrics told stories of high adventure but the last few tones pulled from the instrument sounded like a dirge.

All at once the three men sprang to their feet, for through one of the little windows rising over the edge of the slope appeared three enormous heads. The smoke and smell of the forge had brought word to their enemies. The fight had come to them.

With no time to dress in armor, offensive weapons were taken up without word. Each man embraced the other two, said goodbye, and sprang towards the door. They paused to ask Wulfric, motionless upon his pedestal, for a blessing. Brendan bent and kissed the stately inanimate hand before exiting.

Entering the castle yard, each gave a little distance to the other two so as not to encumber their motions. None wanted the shame of being felled by a friendly sword thrust. The triple giant brotherhood drew near, twice the height of a man and armed to the teeth. Through the visors of giant helmets, monstrous eyes shone with a horrible ferocity.

Each aggressor chose as opponent the man closest to him. Finnian was in the middle position and spied that his adversary's body armor was somewhat clumsily made. Overlapping steel in the lower parts had more play than necessary and Finnian hoped this flaw would give him opportunity. He stood his ground until his foe came near enough to aim a blow at him. A gargantuan mace the size of a weaver's beam came crashing. Finnian leapt aside, and let the blow fall upon the rocky spot where a moment before he had been standing. The giant, full of fury, lunged at him again but Finnian kept eluding the blows and thus began to fatigue his attacker.

The giant took no thought of a counter-assault. The ease of living unmolested in Wittan castle had not taught him to fear. Finnian watched his motions closely, avoiding his blows and becoming attuned to every joint in his armor. At length, the giant stopped to draw his enormous weight up and take in a deep breath. Finnian bounded forward and ran his rapier right through the armor of his opponent's back. He let go the hilt leaving the blade where it stuck and stepped clear as the giant fell. With one blow of his saber, Finnian divided the band of the giant's helmet making way for a second cut across the eyes. The giant was blinded, then beheaded. Uninjured, he turned to see how the brothers had fared. Both of the other giants were down, but so were Dunstan and Brendan. The pairs of combatants were locked together as in a death struggle.

Finnian flew to Dunstan, who had buried his battle-axe in the body of his foe and had fallen beneath him as he toppled. He was alive but in need of aid. After applying a tourniquet from his torn shirt, Finnian went to Brendan.

Brendan had nearly hewn off the left leg of his enemy. Then, while they rolled together on the earth, he had found his dagger and stabbed the giant mortally in the throat. The blood was yet pouring over Brendan's noble hand. The giant had strangled Brendan in his own death agonies. The beautiful slender body lay silent and dead, the fair skin grew yet fairer, and his hazel eagle-eyes no longer shone fierce.

FINNIAN CARRIED THE WOUNDED DUNSTAN into the castle where he washed his lacerations and bound his broken wrist. As he gave his patient drink and made him comfortable, Finnian could not bear to tell him of Brendan's death. But the older brother seemed to know. He did not cast about searching for the third warrior but lay silent and strangely peaceful, cooperating unquestioningly with Finnian's ministrations, fighting nothing, asking nothing.

When Dunstan slept, Finnian returned to the yard to survey the battlefield. As he passed Wulfric standing on his ebony pedestal, he hummed a single bar. But the statue did not move. Not a quiver came in response from the marble man. Having received Brendan's kiss before battle, Wulfric chose affinity with the newly dead.

Strewn upon the yard was death, a glorious death, but four corpses all the same. Finnian's songs could not reach Brendan now any more than they could awaken Wulfric. Finnian felt that to be alive against a backdrop of death was to be out of sync with place and time. While grief was uncomplicated by regret—for his friend had embraced his chosen trial and had not failed in any facet of his quest—Finnian felt thin and ghostlike. Brendan, the true-hearted, was no more. Finnian, the neophyte, lived on.

When Finnian looked down on the mighty form of the giant that lay dead by his own hand, he felt an unfamiliar satisfaction. Perhaps Brendan would forgive him the feelings of pride that arose in his bosom. True, his giant had been a blunderer. Still, the felling of this cruel thick-headed oaf was a commendable deed. He had done something worth doing.

23

Splattered All In Red

THE NEXT MORNING FINNIAN LEFT THE DEAD and injured, and hastened to rouse the village down the hill below Biscop. He needed help to move the heavy carcasses.

A great crowd of peasants came bringing wagons to cart the giants away. Finnian hardly noticed the commotion, celebration, and congratulations. The villagers were eager to claim the unwieldy bodies, arguing among themselves which route would be best for a grand parade throughout the countryside. There were plans for a spectacular procession—Wittan was liberated and all of Capgrave would celebrate.

Hearing a rumor that the king had just arrived at Biscop Palace with a great entourage, Finnian asked a young lad to bear a message.

Dear Sire,

On the palace's westernmost outpost three giants have been felled at high cost. Your noble son Brendan lies dead. Your noble son Dunstan is wounded, but I do not believe mortally. I remain with them both until you give order.

Their servant, your servant,

Finnian

Finnian watched the boy scurry down through the forest path and was glad he could not read. He then turned towards the organized chaos among the carts. He was ready to be alone.

Before the excited company departed, Finnian searched the giants and found the keys of Wittan. He pulled three temperate men from the enthusiastic fray and entrusted them with the task of going with all speed to the castle turned prison. No time was to be wasted in setting free the captives from the cruelties they had suffered at the hand of the giants.

Finally, the crowd departed and Finnian returned to his friends in the tower. There he sat between the dead and the wounded, knowing those better at healing and burial would arrive at any hour. The fellowship of the forges had been overthrown by death and victory. A grateful kingdom would come banging at the gates.

Finnian tried to make wise use of the small window of quiet space, but his soul had never before been so shocked by violence and death. His mind danced disoriented, back and forth between the sacred and mundane. His shoes had tracked in mud. His shirt was splattered in blood. Dunstan labored to breathe. Brendan breathed no more. The thoughts became a song but he could not sing it . . . would not . . . should not—

> *Shirt bespeckled with my blood*
> *Filth upon the floor*
> *Dunstan lies in groaning pain*
> *Brendan is no more*

Finnian's mind then danced away to the ladies waiting in the palace. Ciara had only recently been made whole and hopeful. He, having failed to keep her beloved safe, could not seem to fulfill any of her pleadings. He could not bear to think of what she would do with the shards of a broken heart.

He thought instead of Lenora—lovely Lenora. Would she esteem him now as a comrade in arms to her brave husband? Would she and Dunstan both cease to trouble themselves over his vile fearfulness now that he was a slayer of giants and not just a singer to statuary?

Finnian kicked the remains of the broken cup Brendan had shattered upon the floor on their first night of friendship.

Remembering the impassioned desire for justice, Finnian forgot all *would* and *should*, and sang now simply because he could—

> *Grief o'er fills the ladies' hearts*
> *Brendan now lies dead*

Did I indeed fulfill my part?
Splattered all in red

But song-making brought no relief. And neither Wulfric nor Brendan could be brought back from deep peaceful inanimate rest. Dunstan was just as still.

Finnian's song changed to silent crying as he remembered the fierce hazel eyes of Brendan, "My brother, you were very dear to me. Your love for me was wonderful, more wonderful than that of the great Beech. Though she saved and welcomed me, your comradeship has become my deliverance."

HELP DID ARRIVE LONG BEFORE SUNDOWN, and the private griefs and ponderings of Finnian's inner world were permeated. He was no longer needed as nursemaid or guardian of the fallen. Stumbling back through the dark towards the palace, he found his room was waiting for him. He stripped and climbed between fresh linens.

Over the next few weeks came both the blur of a funeral and the joyful release of Wittan's victims. Intense elation came upon the entire kingdom even while tears were shed for the loss of a beloved prince.

Joy and pride in the deeds of his sons overcame much of the grand old king's sorrow. In magnificent ceremony, he dubbed Finnian a knight with his own old hand in which trembled the sword of his youth. Afterward, the ladies of the court seemed to think it only their duty to make Sir Finnian's life as pleasant as possible. Finnian yielded to their will, swimming with them in the fount, acting out grandiose romantic plays in the library. His meals were delivered to his room once again—now by multiple competing hands.

Surrounded by pleasure's constant distractions, Finnian began to be haunted by his old shadow. In the company of Brendan and Dunstan, consumed by work, he had neither felt nor seen the dark presence, but now he saw it flit in and out of the hallways of Biscop at every turn. Weary, he cast about for an escape from all entanglements.

Sir Dunstan had ridden out into the neighboring kingdom to fight dragons a fortnight earlier, and Sir Finnian decided to follow. Adorned in a splendid suit of armor inlaid with silver given to him by the king, mounted upon a rippling white stallion which was also a gift, he took his leave. It seemed a matter of course that a giant-slayer should next tangle with the winged demons.

During preparations for his new endeavor, Finnian's shadow hid from view, a sure sign to Finnian that he was taking the right course. With its disappearance, a wonderful elevation of spirits came. He began to reflect on his prowess in combat, and forgot now and then that he had only killed *one* of the giants. He began to believe that it was by his initiative that the three had decided to go to battle. Had not his songs been inspiration for the skill and courage of all three warriors?

Sir Finnian began to count himself among the resplendent knights of old. This belief was affirmed by the citizens who bowed and cheered as he rode from the palace. It was validated by tear-soaked pillows in numerous upstairs bedrooms belonging to feminine hearts who feared he might never return, not to mention the lovely ladies who fainted along the way.

By sunset, the villages and crowds fading behind him, Finnian drew near to the forest once again. The first oaks he passed were the advance guard of a dense wood. Soon the trees grew thicker, their trunks pulling together side by side in impenetrable ranks, bodies of rough bark in parade formation. Great boughs arched over the pathway, still as the trunksthat supported them, while high above vacillating leaves swayed frantically at every breath of wind that touched crowded gatherings of foliage. A babbling channel flowed parallel to the forest avenue. Covering the river stones was a tiny forest of moss that mirrored the trees in miniature, swaying under the stream.

*Adorned in a splendid suit of armor, Sir Finnian
took his leave.*

The woods were dense but the pathway for horse and rider was unobstructed. The footsteps of Sir Dunstan had gone before and his stout-hearted spirit still lingered somehow, making a way. Despite the stallion's great stature, Finnian never needed to lower in the least his high-held head.

But as the sun began to set, the shadow descended upon him.

Now Finnian could hardly couch his lance he trembled so. The rattling of his armor was the only noise banging in the surrounding silence except for his horse's hoofbeats. The metallic clamor unnerved his otherwise obedient mount.

Rounding the bend, horse and rider came upon a covered bridge and, though its archway provided ample room for passage, the stallion would not enter. It reared and bucked and stomped. The knight dismounted and attempted to lead the unhinged animal on foot, but the pair were out on their first adventure together and there was not sufficient bond between them to overcome the invading fear.

No amount of cajoling or cursing, or combination thereof, would convince the horse to enter under the archway. At last, the white beast yanked the reins from his rider's hands and cantered off to return home in time for evening oats.

The empty saddle brought distress to the Biscop stable hands, and a rumor went out that dragons were closer by than first presumed. Their brave champion, Sir Finnian, had fallen. Vigil was kept at Brendan's grave asking for his safe return.

24

Sir Finnian Finds His Courage

FINNIAN STOOD ON HIS OWN TWO TREMBLING FEET before the covered bridge. All his fleeing horse's fears became his own. The arcing branches curved round the oval roof, extending its cavernous shape high into the treetops, a carnivorous mouth ready to devour. Finnian could not discern how long and deep the tunnel stretched out before him. The darkness of the surrounding forest crowded the passageway end to end. But the persistent shadow behind him loomed blacker than the tunnel before him and it pressed the horseless knight onward. Finnian entered. His shadow followed.

As he felt his way forward, the sound of the stream flowing over the river stones gurgled underneath the floor of the ancient bridge. Seamless and masterfully built, it did not sag under his footfall. Not a creak sounded in the give-and-take of the wooden trusses in spite of the weight of a man in armor. Finnian found the bridge was no more than ten paces deep, but the exit at the other end was blocked by an iron door. Turning around, he felt his way back. A second door of iron had been closed behind him.

Nothing, not a creature, not so much as spider, mite, or moth abode inside the enclosure except for Finnian and his corrosive companion. The oaken walls rose right up to the roof. Light streamed through a little square opening in the ceiling no bigger than a man's hand. But by this feeble light, no exit could be found. Daylight was in short supply in the deep of the forest. The night came quickly and Finnian sat down on the floor in utter wretchedness.

He slept for some hours and, when he awoke, the moon was taking her turn shooting beams through the hole above. As she rose higher and higher, her light crept down the wall stealthily seeking the prisoner's face. With her touch, the bridge walls appeared to vanish away like a mist, and Finnian found himself again sitting beneath a beech on the edge of a forest. Open country lay in the moonlight for miles around. In the glimmering, he spotted houses, spires, and chimneys. Oh, joy! the horrid prison-bridge was only a dream, thought Finnian, and I have awakened beneath a beech tree, one that loves me perhaps. And I can go where I will. Finnian rose and walked about but could not bring himself to lose sight of the tree. He stayed near the comfort of her presence, waiting for the sun to rise before renewing his journey.

But as soon as the first pale light of the dawn appeared, shadows stole like fainting ghosts through the little square hole above his head. The walls of the covered bridge came back solid, and the glorious night was swallowed up by hateful day. The Beech tree and all her love had evaporated with the dew, and in her stead, Finnian's shadow lay black on the floor beside him.

Thus trapped within the bridge, Finnian lost all of sense of time except the coming and going of sun and moon in the little hole above him. When the night came, the moon's rays touched and freed him. When she left, he was imprisoned by the cruel sun. Every night the conviction returned, that he was at liberty, but could not leave the comfort of the beech. Every morning he sat wretched and disconsolate.

SOMEWHERE IN THE SEQUENCE OF NIGHTS AND DAYS, Finnian recalled how Dunstan had implored him not to follow. He had approached as an equal, knight to knight, asking his friend to remain at the palace and strengthen Oda and comfort Ciara. Dunstan's words had fallen to the floor unheeded. Now Finnian was trapped in the dark, his shadow dancing before him in all its catastrophic vileness. It leapt with glee at the cyclical struggle he could not seem to vanquish. All past victory now tasted to him like sawdust.

A single sentence from the lady of the grass hut leapt into his remembrance, "Corrosive shadows must be slain before dragons and giants." Her warning of something worse had come to fruition. But how does a man slay a shadow—his own shadow? The creature had woven itself into his soul. It was he himself, but braver and fiercer.

Finnian now excoriated his whole history. He had gone out questing not to save the kingdom, but because he was a coward. He could face neither the onerous grief of Ciara nor the uncompromising standards of Oda. He had galloped away full-armored to escape as well from the way his heart soared and sorrowed when he caught sight of Lenora. What might he say if given one moment alone with her?

The shadow snickered.

Finnian hurled forth venom, "What do you know of love, creature?! You who skulk about saying nothing, doing nothing, following and killing everything I touch!"

"What do *you* know of love, creature?" came the hissing, echoing reply.

Finnian would have run his shadow through if it had substance to receive such a wound. He would have cursed him, and indeed opened his mouth to do so, but suddenly he was brought up short. Indeed, what *did* he know of love? What did he know of *Lenora*? Other than his gazing upon her as she lay still encased in marble, besides the words he overheard spoken quietly to her husband in the fountain room, what did he know of Lenora—the flesh-and-blood woman? He loved her symmetrical beauty. He loved his saving of her. He loved ideas of how she might show gratitude for her rescue.

For the next hour, Finnian wept over the truth. His heart did not love but harbored only the possessive lusting after the beauty of a well-made thing. He had not freely granted a human soul her liberty. What did he know of love?

"You are right, my shadow. I do not love Lenora. Nor have I ever."

The shadow shrank and held its peace.

That night, while the half-moon scattered but few thin spectral rays upon him, Finnian dreamed of an autumn night on a hill overlooking his childhood home. His sisters ran to him and took him in their arms. Old friends came flocking round.

But then the sunbeams came and he remembered the boundaries of the trap he had willingly walked into. His brokenness laid claim all over again. The invasion of his sisters into his dreams brought Oda to the forefront of his mind. Lenora had flitted from him like an ethereal forest fairy and Oda had intruded like a maid with a mop bucket. He had found and freed Lenora from her marble encasement. Oda had found and freed him from a tangle of curtains. One woman made him feel like a conquering hero, the other a failing school boy. Again and again Oda drew back the curtain on his true nature, strengths, and struggles.

The truth divided him sharply to his marrow and the shadow cowered. But Finnian, exhausted, slid towards despondency.

Where now was his power of song? If he could call upon the gift, might even his shadow change to something bright and beautiful? He stilled and quieted himself, waiting to see what music might come. All complexity of soul floated up through the hole in the roof as he remembered and believed—the old woman in the grass hut with the young eyes knew something, something she could not tell. And while thinking of her ageless eyes, a song did come—but not from within. A beautiful soft melody came wafting down through the opening above.

The song pierced Finnian through with visions of the tragedy left in his wake. He had first heard the music pressed within the bounds of Ciara's globe and now it came through the warm air in sweet soprano. He had heard its beauty hushed within the wings of the palace, but had paid it no mind. Ciara had told him she was a singer now, but he had never asked to hear. The pomp of knighthood had robbed him of the joy of knowing another—another who held a gift akin to his own. He, after all, was the singing warrior known throughout the kingdom. And she . . . besides the daughter of an elven mother . . . who *was* she?

Finnian had no one to confess to but his shadow, so to the dark fiend he poured out yet another humbling revelation. Mid-phrase, his confession became a song. His whole frame quivered with the joyfully surprised sensation of the unforeseen as his well-rounded tenor joined the soprano outside.

The song of Ciara entered his prison-house—

> *What surge of feeling at the start!*
> *Just come awake, I start to say . . .*
> *And you stop me half the way*
> *As though a veil did cloak your heart.*
> *Is there some gap I leave unmet?*
> *Some outward failed prerequisite*
> *And then I wonder with regret*
> *Have you begun to know me yet?*
> *The petals shut wish to unfold*
> *In seeing them, do you refuse?*
> *Or do you see but what you choose*
> *Does botany obscure the rose?*

Each tone folded its wings, and laid itself, like a caressing bird, upon his heart. Finnian wept yet again, but not for long. He dashed away the tears and moved to the door. There he seated himself and pressed his ear against iron, straining to catch every syllable of the continuing music. The singer seemed to be quite near the covered bridge and to be singing only for him.

Hardly knowing what he did, Finnian reached for the handle above his head. With barest pressure, the latch gave way and the door swung open. He stepped out into the sunshine and there in the road stood Ciara. She smiled, gave a low bow, and turned to begin her return journey. As she departed, she began to sing again in sweet high tones—

> *Deflate my roar of loud protest*
> *And cast the demon Shameful out*
> *And vain Rejection I will rout*
> *Come from my monstrous neediness*
> *What, in the strength of human flesh*
> *With endless struggle, think to gain?*
> *The fearful root does still remain*
> *In spite of all one's willfulness*
> *The fool I was, I could not see*
> *For white-washed walls hid all the grime*
> *I thought to hold and choose my time*
> *But Wisdom smashes dignity*

Finnian remained where he stood, one step outside, watching her leave as one watches a sunset. He sang out harmony, the only thanks he could think of, until he heard her no more.

When she was completely out of sound and sight, Finnian scurried away from the bridge into a nearby thicket, not from shame or fear of being found out, but from sheer terror that, in some evil moment of weakness, he would enter back into the prison-house. In the bushes he stripped off all his armor, the golden spurs, the resplendent mail, and piled it like cordwood under a nearby tree. Greatly lightened, he stood straight and said out loud to himself, "I am what I am, nothing more."

The shadow was nowhere to be seen.

25

Sir Dunstan Gains a Squire

FINNIAN HAD MOVED JUST OUT OF SIGHT of the hated bridge when a voice of another sort sounding through the trees reached his ears. A deep baritone, clear and melodious, sprang from an approaching knight armed from head to heel. Wanting to see who sang now, Finnian crossed the creek and sidled out of the woods between a narrow column of the arching trees. He found himself faced with a bay horse's backside.

Fastened by its long neck to the hinder part of a horse's saddle, the body of a great dragon trailed its hideous length on the ground behind. The horrid, serpent-like head with its black and red forked tongue hanging out of its jaws dangled against the horse's flank, the enormity of its weight causing the horse to make slow progress. The dragon's neck was covered with long blue hair, its sides with scales of green and gold, its back with corrugated skin of purple hue. Its belly was also contracted with wrinkles and folds, but the color was leaden, dashed with blotches of livid blue. Skinny, bat-like wings and tail were a shimmering grey. The gorgeous colors, curving lines, iridescent wings, silken hair, and opalescent scales combined to form intense ugliness.

Finnian stepped towards the side of the horse near where the foot of the knight hung loosely next to the silver stirrup. There had been a time when he could have kissed the boot for the simple fact that Lenora loved the man wearing it. Now, his heart was captivated by the presence of a dragon slayer. Sir Dunstan reined up and looked down. Finnian also looked down. In as few words as possible, he offered himself as a squire.

Dunstan wanted to dismount and throw his arms around his comrade, but he stayed in the saddle and spoke softly, holding out his gauntleted right hand, "Squire and knight should be friends." He wondered, but did not ask, where the silver armor was and the white stallion given by his father. Before him stood a man that had been made, at great cost, to renounce what he himself was able to daily take up and bear with great joy. Dunstan knew, without knowing how he knew, that another soul's journey was not his to comprehend.

Finnian grasped the offered hand with gratitude and no more was said. Dunstan gave the sign to his horse to renew the slow march. Finnian walked beside and a little behind the draggling mangled serpent.

THAT EVENING THE TWO TRAVELERS ARRIVED at a little cottage and, with no warning or word of greeting, a woman rushed out crying, "My child! My child! Have you found my little girl?"

"I did find her," replied Sir Dunstan with great calm. "I left her with the hermit quite injured, though I do think, in time, she will recover."

The mother, cloak in hand, rushed headlong out into the woods towards the hermit's hut. She was almost out of sight when her husband came to the doorway. Speechless thanks overtook his entire countenance.

Dunstan reached back and undid the bindings on the dragon's neck saying, "As you can see, I have brought you a present." The frightful burden fell with a great thud.

"You must bury the monster," added Dunstan, "or there will be an unspeakable stench."

The husband nodded and his eyes widened in horror as he surveyed the monstrous beast.

Dunstan dismounted, put a hand on the man's shoulder, and said assuringly, "If I had arrived a moment later, I should have been too late, but now you need not fear."

"Are there more about?" whispered the man, quaking slightly, a question that would have never crossed his lips had his wife been present. In her absence he wanted the unvarnished truth.

"A creature like this one is rare, but if there is a swarm of them, I've never heard of one appearing in the same neighborhood where a relative is buried."

"First thing tomorrow then, I'll start digging," said the peasant, greatly relieved. "The villagers will help when they hear it is a deterrent." Then, remembering his manners, he said, "Will you not come in and rest, Sir Dunstan?"

"That I will, thank you," replied the knight, handing the reins to his squire. Dunstan directed Finnian to unbridle the horse and lead him into the shelter of a great tree several paces off. "You need not tie him up," he instructed. "He will not run away."

Finnian did more than unbridle. Finding a brush and hoof pick in the baggage, he removed saddle and blanket, bridle and harness, and groomed the steed from stem to stern. The horse leaned in grateful for every stroke as the smell of dragon was whisked away into the night wind. Finnian kissed his wide velvety nostrils for the simple fact he belonged to Sir Dunstan.

Horse re-saddled and bridle hung, Finnian made his way to the cottage threshold. He leaned against the doorway and looked into the room filled with warm firelight. His knight, helmet removed, was engrossed in conversation with the simple host. Here shone the heart of the man Lenora loved. A nobler countenance Finnian had never seen. Goodwill beamed from every line of his haggard face. Arduous combat did not veil the gentle heart. Finnian was motioned to come and sit. All three supped and fell into satisfied reverie.

Silence held sway until the mother returned with the wounded child in her arms. The all-but-dead face was white from blood loss and terror. The woman was as pale as her little burden, wild with love and despairing tenderness.

Dunstan rose. The light that had been confined to his eyes, now shone from his whole countenance, stern and determined, all but fierce. He took the little girl in his arms and, with the mother's help, undressed her and looked to her lacerations. The powerful hands turned and shifted, pressed and bound as gently as the woman's, tears flowing down his face as he did so. He bent and kissed the pale cheeks before mother tucked her into her bed and made sure the lady had eaten before beginning the long night watch.

The next morning, with a few parting instructions as to how to continue treatment of the little patient, knight and squire took their leave. Finnian brought Dunstan his steed, held the stirrup while he mounted, and followed him on foot into the wood. The horse, delighted to be free of his hideous load, bounded beneath the weight of only a man in armor and could hardly be held back from galloping on.

Dunstan restrained him for an hour or two then dismounted. He then compelled his companion to get into the saddle, saying, "The labor must be shared."

Sir Dunstan walked, his hand against the dangling stirrup. Heavily clad as he was, he moved with apparent ease. He bared his heart to Finnian as an equal, "Even with the beauty of this country there is much that is wrong in it. Great splendors, corresponding horrors, heights and depths, beautiful women and awful fiends, noble men and cowards. All a man can do," he said, stroking his chin with his free hand, "is to better what he can."

Finnian listened, and thought, *I* hope for no more than to better *myself.*

Sir Dunstan continued, "I am coming to accept the fact, Finnian, that as I age I will be more often defeated. It cannot be helped. In any case, renown and success are of no great value. I must finish the work allotted to me and do my best to keep an even temper and strong will. Life, as a whole, is a steady plodding."

Steady plodding was something Finnian could grasp. His hunger for ecstasy had led to enslavement, and he was ready for the freedom discipline might bring. Since he had no more ambition to *be* a knight, his service *to* his knight intensified in its wholeheartedness. He tended Sir Dunstan's horse and cleaned his armor, using his skill in metal craft to repair it when necessary. He saw to Dunstan's needs with all vigilance and was well repaid in love and companionship, but he hardly noticed. All he knew was that his heart was glad.

The two journeyed towards home where the women who loved them prayed for their return. They rested at night in whatever shelter was offered or lay in the forest under great trees on couches of old leaves.

26

Dark Knowledge Put to Use

TWO DAYS' JOURNEY FROM HOME, the appearance of newly-made roads in the woods came into view. Branches had been cut down and openings widened. Dunstan and Finnian came into a long, narrow avenue, formed by the felling of trees whose freshly exposed gnarled roots gave evidence. In less than an hour, the path brought them to a dead end. A wall of yew trees grew high and so close together that their branches intertwined like plaited hair. Nothing could be seen beyond the barrier. Not far off the path, a curious opening was cut in the interlocking trunks like a door, smooth and perpendicular, just high enough for a man to pass through. Dunstan dismounted, Finnian tethered his horse, and the two entered the place together.

Stepping inside, they saw four great walls of yew enclosing a wide rectangular space. Along the two longer sides stood three ranks of men in white robes at sober silent attention. Except for their swords, their attire was priestly. In the center of the arena was a silent crowd of men, women, and children from the surrounding villages, dressed in holiday attire.

In the ever-increasing darkness, the stars shining down into the enclosure grew brighter and larger. The pinnacles of the treetops swayed in the wind vibrating—half like music, half like moaning.

Dunstan leaned towards Finnian and whispered, "How solemn this is. Surely the people wait to hear the voice of a prophet. Something wondrous is near!"

Finnian stared about. He wanted to concur, but could not. With growing unease, he adopted a heightened watchfulness, and held his peace.

Just then a bright star appeared high overhead, illuminating the area throughout. A four-part fortissimo harmony soared from the white robes, modulating as it rolled like thunder round and round the enclosure. Now receding to one end, now approaching the other, the wall of sound passed from one chorus of twelve to the next in great crescendos.

The song paused, and a company of six priests marched up the center aisle surrounding a youth. He was gorgeously attired and wearing a chaplet of flowers upon his head. They moved in slow march towards a platform upon which sat a throne, high above the heads of the surrounding crowd. The priests and the young man began to ascend a gentle slope.

Upon the platform sat a throne, high above the heads of the surrounding crowd.

On the elevated throne sat a majestic figure whose posture bespoke both pride and loving condescension. He looked down on the multitude as the company ascended to the foot of his throne and knelt. The youth was then seated at the potentate's feet and a benign right hand was placed palm down upon his head, as if to bless. It seemed to Finnian the young man shrank.

There arose a burst of song from the multitude, jubilant and approving. Several choruses of the enchanting melody flowed forth again, modulating and thundering. Again the song paused. Another company of six came forth. Six women robed in white approached the throne surrounding another chosen one. A wreath of flowers was set upon another young brow, and this time, Finnian knew the face.

As the women slowly and steadily advanced up the center aisle, Finnian turned to look at Sir Dunstan. The knight's noble countenance was full of reverence and awe. The grand spectacle had vanquished him: the stars overhead, the towering yew-trees, the wind's sighing moan through their branches. The interlacing strands of breathless beauty had captured the entirety of Dunstan's noble spirit. His humble ignorance of evil hid from him the sense of dread which continued to grow in Finnian.

Finnian had learned much in the company of his shadow. Though powerless, he was not deceived. All he observed he knew to be the deception of witchcraft wrapped in the robes of priesthood. He knew all that unfolded before him was worse than every treachery of Alder and Ash.

To see Sir Dunstan helplessly enrapt by the appearances of solemnity tore at Finnian. The villagers in the crowd had noted their prince's approval and submitted themselves to the ceremony body and soul. Finnian knew that later in the clear light of day, the truth would dawn on Dunstan and the knight would bitterly repent his naive support of a hideous lie.

Helpless to awaken his master, Finnian gave all his focus now to the procession of women. Again, the company ascended to the foot of the throne and knelt. The young woman joined the youth seated at the potentate's feet. When the palm came down upon her scalp she also shrank. In her fear, Finnian found his courage.

Finnian went to his knees in the thick of the stooping crowd. He moved forward, rising up and kneeling down in the undulating habit of the worshippers, only he never knelt in the same place twice. He made his way through the singing, genuflecting flock all the way to the front. Questioning looks overshadowed the faces he passed but his unswerving confidence gave passage. Indifference to his own fate provided a pervading fearless calm. In minutes he stood at the foot of the platform.

The song had just ceased and Finnian felt the eyes of many looking towards him. Instead of yet another scuttling kowtow, Finnian stood straight and walked right up the stairs to the throne. Disbelief paralyzed all looking on, Dunstan among them, as Finnian laid hold of the demigod by the scruff of his neck and threw him tumbling down the wide steps. He next took hold of the throne itself and strained with all his might. A cracking, breaking, and tearing of rotten wood gave way, and Finnian hurled the seat down the steps after the pretender. Now groups of priests began to rush the stage.

The throne's removal revealed a cavernous hole like the hollow of a decaying tree. Out of its depths rushed an enormous fiend like an immense wolf. The beast knocked Finnian backwards and a tangle of limbs fell headlong tumbling, scraping, and skidding to the base of the platform. As they fell, Finnian caught the monster by the throat and a struggle to the death began. Around them arose wild cries of fury and revenge. A universal hiss of steel rang out as every sword was swept from its scabbard tearing the very air to shreds. Hundreds now rushed into the fray.

But Finnian only tightened his grasp on the brute's throat. Its eyes were already bulging from its head, its tongue dangling out. Finnian hoped that even after they had run him through, no man could undo his grip on the beastly throat. He threw all his will, and force, and purpose into both grasping hands.

Finnian did not feel the blows. A faintness came over him, and all consciousness departed.

27

A Proper Knightly Burial

Dunstan and Lenora, Oda, and Ciara wept over him. Their tears fell on Finnian's face before the casket closed.

Brendan greeted him with open arms.

"Ah!" said Dunstan to his fellow mourners, "I rushed among them like a madman. I hewed them down like brushwood. Their swords battered on him like hail while I cut a lane through to my friend. He was dead. But he had throttled the monster. Oda and I had to cut a handful out of the beast's throat before we could disengage his hands and carry off his body. No false priest dared molest us as we brought him back."

"He died well," sighed Lenora.

They bore him to his grave and laid him within the grounds of Biscop Palace amid many trees. Finnian felt the coffin settle on the firm earth and heard the sound of the falling dirt upon its lid. He lay in earth's bosom, his soul a motionless lake, receiving all things and, for the moment, giving nothing back. The footsteps of his friends above sent a thrill through his heart. He felt like a tired child laid down in his white bed, the sound of playthings being put aside for the night.

Oda remained and spoke low, gentle, tearful words to him who lay beneath the wounded sod. "You saved me. I thought to draw my final breath. But, in the end, you loved and saved me."

Finnian rose into a single large primrose that grew by the edge of the grave and from the petaled window looked out upon the countenance of Oda. The flower caught her eye. She stooped and plucked it, saying, "Oh, you beautiful creature!" and, lightly kissing it, put it in the buttonhole near her bosom.

As the sun went below the horizon, rosy beams illuminated a feathery cloud that floated high above the world. Finnian withdrew from the flower and threw himself upon it and floated in sight of the sinking sun.

The sun's rose hue shone on, loving without needing to be loved in return. And Finnian now knew it was by loving, and not by being loved, that one can come nearest the soul of another.

The moon came gliding up, holding all his past in her wan face. She changed Finnian's feathery couch into a ghostly pallor, and threw her light on the earth below as to the bottom of a pale sea of dreams.

Ah! my friends, Finnian thought, how I will tend you, and haunt you with my love. You will see me in statues' tears and smell me in the air like myrrh. Aggrieved old women, worn out men, and forgotten children, how I will wait on you and minister to you. I will put my arms about you in the dark and think hope into your hearts when you imagine no one is near. As soon as my senses have all come back, and have grown accustomed to this new blessed life, I will be among you with the love that heals.

Of all the friends that listened, Ciara heard Finnian's voice most clearly. The next morning she set out with money for two commissions.

Forty days later, in a faraway kingdom, a master craftsman of marble received patronage for two tall and stately statues. The lady who handed him gold described the forms of two fallen knights loved dearly. When he completed his artful task, he wrapped each with care, crated them with tenderness, and sent them out by wagon towards the Palace of Biscop. Two empty ebony pedestals awaited them on either side of the entryway.

28

Finnian Returns

F INNIAN SANK BACK INTO THE WORLD of his birth. He lay in the open air in the early morning before sunrise and over him rose the summer sky. He slowly got to his feet and found himself on the summit of a little hill. A valley lay beneath, and a range of mountains encompassed the far horizon.

He yawned, stretched, and then his heart jumped in panic—for from his feet a huge expanding shape stretched across the valley. There it lay, long and large, dark and mighty. His shadow had followed him home! Filled with revulsion and dread, Finnian braced himself to be overcome by the familiar dark presence.

Then, to his immense relief, Finnian noticed the sun had just lifted itself above the eastern hill. The darkness that fell was only the natural shadow that goes with every man who walks the earth on a cloudless day. He danced in ecstatic joy.

Rapturously delivered from his deepest fear, Finnian's heart settled and he began to recognize the country around him. In the valley below lay his home and the haunts of childhood. He felt within a power of calm endurance new to him, a depth of peace bringing ineffable delight. He knew that an hour of such peace made all the turmoil of a lifetime worth striving through.

By midmorning he had reached the garden gate and there his sisters received him with unspeakable joy. They had been in great distress about him since he first disappeared twenty-one days previous. To Finnian it had seemed twenty-one years.

His siblings, after several attempts, ceased asking for an explanation. It was enough that he was home. He seemed no worse for the wear, whatever had befallen him. And both women, despite being his elders, observed a new depth to him that elicited a respect, even a slight touch of awe. In less than a fortnight both released to him the role of leadership over the entire family estate.

Finnian was not so quick to trust himself and his own perceptions. Each night when he lay down once more in his own bed, he never felt certain that when he awoke he would not find himself again in Biscop serving Sir Dunstan, or wandering the woods of Capgrave dodging his shadow. His dreams were incessant and perturbed and each morning he looked round to see that he was indeed at his boyhood home in his own bed.

As Finnian began the slow plodding duties of his new position, his mind calmed. He was not sure if, or how, all he learned in Capgrave, Biscop, and all the forest in-between translated into common life. He wondered if he must live it all over again, and learn it all over again, in the forms that belonged to the world of men.

For weeks he found himself peering round to see how his shadow fell. And, though he cast no more or less shade on the earth than any man his size, he had a strange feeling sometimes that he was a ghost—sent into the world to minister or at least to repair the wrongs he had already done.

Finnian found the blessedness he experienced after his burial at Biscop too wondrous to lay hold upon. When he thought of the wise woman in the hut by the sea, a sadness would possess him, but it would change to joy as he remembered her solemn assurance that she knew something too good to be told. When he was oppressed by any sorrow or perplexity, he remembered her songs and was comforted by her wise tenderness. He would console himself by saying, "I came back to my home through my tomb. I will return to her through a tomb again one day and be glad."

THAT AUTUMN FINNIAN OVERSAW THE REAPERS. On the third day of harvest, when they ceased their work at noon, he lay down under the shadow of a great, ancient beech tree that stood on the edge of the field. Eyes closed, he began to listen to the sound of the leaves overhead. At first, they made sweet inarticulate music but by and by, the sound took shape, molding itself into words. At last came a couplet, half-dissolved in a little ocean of tones over and over, "A great good is coming—is coming—is coming to thee, Finnian." The sound reminded Finnian of the voice of the ancient woman in the grass hut by the sea. He opened his eyes, and, for a moment, almost believed that he saw her face, with its many wrinkles and its young eyes, looking at him from between two hoary branches of the beech overhead. But when he looked more keenly, he saw only twigs and leaves and the face of a curious blackbird staring down from above. The bird took flight leaving only the infinite sky, in blue spots, gazing through between. Yet he knew that good *was* coming to him—that good is always coming—though he had only in moments possessed the simplicity and the courage to believe it.

Appendix I

A Finnian Favorite

FINNIAN LUDWELL HAS SEVEN FAVORITE BOOKS. *Ceolfrith and the Mirror* is third in preference.[11] The work has been condensed below.[12]

When Finnian first read *Ceolfrith and the Mirror* in the tenth grade, he gushed about it in his private journal as follows—

> *It is just as a fairy book should be. Like silver veins go branching through hard rock, it glows and flashes thoughts upon my soul. While I read it, I am Ceolfrith, and his history is mine.*

Finnian was the kind of boy who needed to be careful about what he read. But he was not. Before he turned sixteen, he was becoming eccentric.

––––––––––––––––––

[11] Among his other favorites of course were *The Ring of Doom, In Light of the New Moon,* and *Walter and the Raven.*

[12] Originally 95,022 words, the story is now a manageable 6,000, or thereabouts. I'm sure Gutenberg.org has it in all its unabridged glory.

Ceolfrith and the Mirror

I saw a ship sailing upon the sea
Deeply laden as ship could be;
But not so deep as in love I am
For I care not whether I sink or swim.
—Old Ballad

CEOLFRITH VON HUBERT WAS A STUDENT at a respected university. Though of a noble family, he was poor, but said he did not care. "Poverty means independence," he bragged regularly. Indeed, having no money meant he had none to lose.

Ceolfrith was a favorite with his fellow students but had yet to make a friend. The secret of his popularity was the safe harbor of his retreat. None of his peers had ever crossed the threshold of his lodging, an attic room in an old house near the center of town. His unknown abode gave him an air of mystery. And every evening, he knew he would be gloriously alone and undisturbed to read and dream to his heart's content. When he looked down from his window on the street below, each man and maiden moved as in a tale unfolding in his own mind. But Ceolfrith was a poet without words. The springing waters were dammed back into his soul, where, finding no utterance, they grew, and swelled, and threatened to undermine.

At the university, Ceolfrith embraced some subjects not entirely approved by his elders and certainly not mainstream. The history of the occult and the quest for the philosopher's stone were favorite topics of reading. But it was simply idle curiosity; Ceolfrith was not a believer, much less a practitioner in these matters.

His lodging consisted of one large low-ceilinged room, bare of furniture except for a couple of wooden chairs, a couch which served for dreaming on both by day and night, and a wardrobe of black oak. Oddities hung about in each corner. In one stood a skeleton, half leaning against the wall, half supported by a string about its neck. One of its hands rested on the heavy pommel of a great sword that stood beside. Various weapons were scattered over the floor. On the west wall hung a large dried bat with wings spread. Next to it was the skin of a porcupine, and below that a stuffed sea-mouse. These pieces of decor had only interested Ceolfrith for a day or two—his mind still lay like twilight open to any wind. He had yet to find an absorbing passion or a sense of calling.

The young bachelor would lie on his couch and read a tale or a poem until the book dropped from his hand. Thus he would segue from daydream to sleeping fantasy often not knowing whether he was awake or asleep, until the gold in the sunrise flashed upon the ceiling. He would arise, go out, and keep active in study or sport until the close of the day left him free. Then the world of night again rose up in his soul, with all its stars, and dim-seen phantoms. But the inertia of Ceolfrith's well-ordered life could not be maintained forever. Time has a way of bringing swift consequences and hard decisions.

One afternoon, towards dusk, he was wandering dreamily along one of the main streets of town when a fellow student roused him by a slap on the shoulder. The acquaintance asked Ceolfrith to accompany him into a little back alley shop to look at some old armor he was considering purchasing. Ceolfrith was thought by his fellow students to be an authority in every matter pertaining to arms, ancient or modern. In the use of weapons, none of his peers could come near him, and he went along willingly as the established expert.

The two entered a narrow alley, traveling through a dirty little court, under a low arched doorway, and into a miscellaneous assortment of everything musty, dusty, and old. After Ceolfrith judged the armor satisfactory and the asking price reasonable, his companion made the purchase. But as the two were leaving the place, Ceolfrith's eye was attracted by an old mirror. Its elliptical shape was framed in curious carving that glimmered in the shop owner's hand-held light. It hung crookedly on a back wall covered with dust. Ceolfrith said nothing and departed with his friend.

The young men walked together to the main street, and parted in opposite directions.

No sooner was Ceolfrith left alone, than the thought of the curious mirror returned to him. A strong desire to study it arose within him and back he went to the shop. The owner—a little, old, withered man with a pocked face —opened the door when he knocked as if he had expected him. The old man's burning eyes were in constant slow restless motion, looking here and there after something that eluded them. Pretending to examine several other articles, Ceolfrith at last approached the mirror and requested to have it taken down.

"Take it down yourself, master, I cannot reach it," said the old man.

Ceolfrith lowered the piece with tender care and saw that the carved frame was delicate and costly. The intricate patterns contained carved knots woven in and out in strands impossible to trace but inviting one to solve the enigma all the same. The young man was sure the pattern held meaning, which increased his longing to possess. He pretended, however, to want it only for practical use and commented that the reflection was rather dull. The shopkeeper made but one swipe with his handkerchief against the surface and his client stood before a brilliant glass uninjured by age, clear and perfect. Ceolfrith asked about the price, feigning indifference. The old man replied with an amount far beyond the reach of the poor bachelor and the young would-be customer turned and lifted the mirror back up to its former place.

"You think the price too high?" inquired the shopkeeper.

"It may be a fair price for you to ask," replied Ceolfrith, "but it is far too much for me to give."

The old man held up his light towards Ceolfrith's face. "I like your look," he said.

Ceolfrith could not return the compliment. In fact, now he that he looked closely at the old man, he felt a kind of repugnance.

"What is your name?" he continued.

"Ceolfrith von Hubert."

"Ah, ah! I thought as much. I see your father in you. I knew your father very well, young sir. I dare say in some odd corners of my shop, you might find some old things with his crest upon them still."

Ceolfrith wondered that his father would have any dealings with the likes of the man who tottered about before him but remained silent. The old man did not. "Well, I like you," he said, "You shall have the mirror at a fourth of the cost, but upon one condition."

"What is the condition?" asked Ceolfrith, the price now barely within his range but his yearning to own the piece exponentially increasing.

"That if you should ever want to get rid of it again, you will let me have the first offer."

"Certainly," replied Ceolfrith with a smile, adding, "a moderate condition indeed."

"On your honor?" insisted the seller.

"On my honor," said the buyer. And the bargain was concluded.

"I will carry it home for you," said the old man.

But Ceolfrith took it in his hands answering, "No, no. I will carry it myself," for he had a peculiar dislike of revealing his residence to anyone, and certainly not to the shopkeeper. His dislike of the old man was steadily increasing and he was eager to leave.

"Just as you please," said the old creature as he held his light aloft at the door, showing his customer out. The light trembled in his hand as he muttered to himself, "Sold for the sixth time. I should think my lady has had enough vain attention by now."

Ceolfrith carried his prize home as if it were delicate china and all the way he had an uncomfortable feeling that he was being followed. Repeatedly he looked about, but saw nothing to justify his suspicions. But the streets were too crowded and dimly lit to know for sure. He reached his lodging in safety and leaned his purchase against the wall, relieved to be rid of its weight. Lighting his pipe, Ceolfrith collapsed upon the couch. There, after a good smoke, he lapsed into dreams.

He returned home earlier than usual the next day after class, determined to affix the mirror to the wall over the hearth at one end of his long room. Before hanging it, he wiped every speck of dust away from its face. Though the looking glass shone out as clear as the water of a sunny spring, Ceolfrith remained occupied with the curious carving of the frame. This he cleaned as well as he could with a brush. Making minute examination of its various parts, in the hope of discovering the intentions and secrets of the carver, his fascination increased, but he came no closer to solving the riddle of its making.

Fatigued, he turned his gaze to the glass and stared vacantly for a few moments into the depth of the reflected room. His room was the same as its reflection, but not. All commonness was gone. His ordinary quarters had become art.

CEOLFRITH LOOKED INTO THE MIRROR at the reflected skeleton and almost feared it. It stood still as a watchtower looking across the waste of the busy world into the quiet regions of the unseen beyond. Ceolfrith knew every bone and every joint in it as well as his own fist. But in the reflection, it looked like it might at any moment catch up an old battle-axe in a mailed hand and, by a mighty arm, bring it crashing down through an armored helmet, slicing skull and brain. "I should like to live in *that* room if I could only get into it," whispered Ceolfrith, stepping towards the mirror.

Scarcely had the half-molded words floated from his mouth when through the door of the reflected room glided noiseless and unannounced the graceful form of a woman. Her steps were reluctant and faltering. Dressed all in white, her back alone was visible as she as she walked to the couch and laid wearily down. She turned, and he beheld a face of unutterable loveliness. Yet suffering and a sense of compulsion mingled with her beauty.

Ceolfrith stood frozen, his eyes fixed upon her. Recovering somewhat, he looked around to face the couch behind him. It was vacant. In bewilderment mingled with terror, he turned again to the mirror. There, on the reflected sofa lay the exquisite lady. Closed eyes veiled tears and she lay still as death except for her labored breathing.

Ceolfrith's emotions were of a kind that destroys consciousness. He was never later able to clearly recall his feelings in that moment. He could not, though he was painfully aware of his rudeness, keep from staring at the lady in the reflection. He feared that she would open her eyes and discover his intrusive gaze. But before long his anxiety lessened, for when her eyes opened blinking and unfocused she never looked in Ceolfrith's direction. She rose and wandered in aimlessness about the room to take stock of her surrounding and he realized then that if she could see him at all, she would see only his back. He also realized that she could only see those items in his room that were reflected in the mirror.

By and by her eyes fell upon the skeleton, and Ceolfrith saw her shudder in repugnance. He would have removed the obnoxious thing at once, but he feared its sudden disappearance would agitate her even more.

So Ceolfrith stood and watched her as the troubled expression faded from her face, leaving only a faint sorrow behind. She resettled herself on the couch, her features relaxing into an unchanging expression of rest. By the slow regular motion of her breathing, Ceolfrith knew she slept and he could gaze on her without embarrassment. Her figure was harmonious, worthy of her face. Her delicately molded feet matched the equally elegant hands. Her simple dress did not distract from her beauty in perfected repose. Ceolfrith gazed till he was weary, and at last seated himself and mechanically took up a book. But like one who watches by a sickbed, he gathered no thoughts from the page before him.

All Ceolfrith's intellect and past experience was stunned by the shocked contradiction. Beyond astonishment, his imagination went wild. He lost track of all time and grew drowsy in reverie. When he roused himself and sat up, trembling from head to toe, he looked again into the mirror. The lady was gone.

The glass reflected faithfully what his room presented, and nothing more. It hung there like a golden jewelry setting with the central gem stolen. She had carried away with her all the wonder of the reflected room. It had sunk again to the level of the commonplace.

After the first pangs of his disappointment had passed, Ceolfrith began to hope. Perhaps the lady would return the next evening at the same hour. Resolving that if she did, she should not at least be scared by the hateful skeleton, he removed it, and several other articles of questionable taste. He tucked them away into a recess by the side of the hearth where they could not possibly cast a reflection into the mirror. Then, having made his poor room as tidy as a bachelor knows how, he went for a walk. The solace of the open sky and the night wind that had begun to blow calmed his nerves somewhat. When he returned to his flat, he could not bring himself to lie down on his bed for she had lain upon its reflection. To sleep there would be sacrilege. But eventually weariness prevailed and Ceolfrith collapsed fully dressed upon the couch until morning.

THE FOLLOWING EVENING with palpitations so fierce he could hardly breathe, Ceolfrith stood in dumb hope before the mirror. Again his reflected room shone as in the gathering twilight, anxious for a coming splendor. As the strokes of the neighboring church bell announced the hour of six, the room vibrated and in glided the pale beauty. Again she laid herself upon the couch. Poor Ceolfrith went half mad with delight. She had returned! Her eyes sought the corner where the skeleton had stood and, seeing it empty, a faint gleam of satisfaction crossed her face.

Emanating less tension than the previous night, she took more notice of the things about her, stopping to gaze with some curiosity at the books and papers strewn about. At length, however, drowsiness overtook her, and again she fell asleep. This time Ceolfrith was resolved to not lose sight of her, but the lady's all absorbing repose passed contagiously from her to him. Hours later, when she moved, he started as if from a dream. He watched her rise and pass from the room, eyes closed, with the gait of a sleepwalker.

In spite of the inexplicableness of his situation, Ceolfrith was in a state of extravagant delight. Most men have a secret treasure somewhere. The miser has his golden hoard, the magician his secret spell, the scholar his rare book, the poet his favorite haunt, but Ceolfrith had a mirror with a lovely lady in it. And now that he knew by her response to the skeleton that she was affected by the things around her, he had a new goal in life: he would turn the portion of his bare chamber reflected in the mirror into a room that any lady would love to call her own.

Ceolfrith was poor but possessed one marketable skill. Until now his pride restrained him from work and he lived on his slender allowance. To do otherwise was to soil the status of his rank. But now he advertised a willingness to give lessons in fencing and swordplay to any who could pay him well for his trouble. His offer, though a surprise to his fellow students, was eagerly accept by many for he was the best swordsman in the university. Soon his instructions were not confined to the richer students, but were anxiously sought by many of the young nobility of the city.

In less than six weeks Ceolfrith had a good deal of money at his command. He purchased muslin screens behind which he hid his tattered couch and a few other necessaries. He stuffed his remaining belongings into a closet. An elegant couch was procured for the lady to lie upon. By every day adding some article of luxury, Ceolfrith converted his poor apartment into a rich boudoir.

Every night, at about the same time, the lady entered. The first time she saw the new couch, she started with a half-smile. Then her face grew very sad and tears came. She laid herself upon the couch and pressed her face into the silken cushions as if to hide. With each addition and change she gave a look of acknowledgment, as if she knew that someone was ministering to her, and wanted to show gratitude. But the look of suffering did not dissipate.

One night, after she had lain down as usual, her eyes fell upon some paintings with which Ceolfrith had just finished adorning the walls. She rose, and to his delight, walked across the room and examined them with pleasure.

But then again the sorrowful expression returned, and she buried her face in the pillows of her couch. Yet over the weeks her countenance began to grow more composed, the suffering became less sharp, and a quiet, hopeful expression took its place.

Meantime Ceolfrith's interest, as might be expected in one of his temperament, had blossomed into love, and his love had ripened, or, more accurately, withered into passion. He tragically bore overpowering affection for a reflection. He could not go near her, could not speak to her, could not hear a sound from her sweet lips. His heart felt ready to break with intensity of longing, and the more he did for her, the more he loved her.

Ceolfrith hoped that, although she never appeared to see him, she knew that one unknown was ready to give his life to her. He tried to comfort himself by thinking that perhaps someday she would see him and make signs to him. He told himself that a single sign would sate his heart. He reasoned, is it not true that the best a loving soul can do is to enter into communion with the other? How many who love never come nearer than I do? How many seem to know and yet never enter the inward life of the other soul? How many part in the end with only the vaguest notion of the Universe on whose borders they have been hovering for years? If I could but speak to her, and know that she heard me, I should be satisfied.

Once he contemplated painting a picture to hang on the wall to convey to the lady a thought of himself. But, though he had some skill, he found his hand trembled so much when he began the attempt that he was forced to give it up.

One evening, as he stood gazing on his treasure, Ceolfrith thought he saw a faint expression of self-consciousness on her countenance, as if she surmised that passionate eyes were fixed upon her. Her self-awareness grew until the red blood rose over her neck and cheek and brow. This particular night she was dressed in an evening costume, resplendent with diamonds. It added nothing to her beauty, but it presented it in a new facet. Diamonds glittered from amidst her hair, half hidden in its luxuriance, like stars through dark rain clouds. Bracelets on her white arms flashed as she lifted her snowy hands to cover her burning face. But her beauty outshone all its adornment. Ceolfrith's longing to approach her became almost delirious.

If I might have but one of her feet to kiss, thought Ceolfrith, I should be content. But he deceived himself, for passion is never content.

Suddenly, as if an arrow had been aimed and driven deep, a thought darted into his mind: She has a lover somewhere. She is thinking of him in her blushing. I am nothing and nowhere to her. She lives in another world after she leaves me.

Ceolfrith paced the floor madly. Why does she come and make me love her, till I, a strong man, grow faint? He looked again, and her face was pale as a lily. A sorrowful compassion rebuked the glitter of the restless jewels, and the slow tears rose in her eyes. She left the room sooner this evening than ever before. Ceolfrith remained alone, his chest empty and hollow with the weight of the whole world crushing in its walls. The next evening, for the first time since she began to come, she made no appearance.

Now Ceolfrith was in a wretched plight. Since the thought of a rival had occurred to him, he could not rest for a moment. More than ever he longed to see the lady face to face. He persuaded himself that if he but knew the worst, he would be satisfied. If she loved another, he would abandon university and find relief in constant travel—the hope of all active minds when invaded by distress.

He waited with unspeakable anxiety for the next night, yearning for her return. When she did not come, he fell ill. He ceased to attend the lectures and his engagements were neglected. He cared for nothing. When for six evenings she did not come, bright sunny skies were pale to him—a heartless, burning desert. The men and women in the streets were mere puppets without motives, having no interest to him. She—she alone and altogether—was his universe, his well of life, his incarnate good. Absorbing passion and slow consuming fever now led to incautious resolutions.

Ceolfrith reasoned that his beloved was somehow enchanted by the mirror. For, he said to himself, a spell forced her presence in that glass. It was clear she came unwillingly at first. So why should not a stronger spell compel her to come to me bodily? His conscience pricked him but he used love as an excuse, saying, I want only to know my doom from her own lips.

Ceolfrith opened his secret drawer in the back side of the wardrobe and took out his books of magic. Lighting his lamp, he began to read. He made notes from midnight till three in the morning, on three successive nights. Then he returned his books to their hiding place and went out in quest of materials necessary for conjuration. They were not easy to find. (The ingredients employed for all incantations of this nature are below the standards of this author to mention.)

Ceolfrith knew touching such materials and using them in connection with his beloved was inexcusable. In order to press forward and quash all pricks of conscience, he compartmentalized, sequestering his heart from his hands. At length all items were procured, and Ceolfrith prepared for the exercise of unlawful and tyrannical power.

He cleared the center of the room, stooped, and drew a circle of red on the floor. Within the ring he wrote four mystical signs and four numbers. All were powers of seven or nine, one in each point of the compass. He examined the whole ring carefully to see that no smallest break had occurred in the marked circumference and straightened up just as the church clock struck seven. Then, just as she had appeared the first time, reluctant, slow, and stately, glided in the reflection of his beloved. Ceolfrith trembled.

She turned and revealed a countenance worn and wan. Ceolfrith grew faint and questioned too late if he dared to proceed. But her face and form now possessed his whole soul, to the exclusion of all other joys and griefs. His longing to speak to her, to know that she heard him, to hear from her one word in return, became so unendurable that he resolved to follow through.

Stepping carefully from the circle, he brought a small incense burner into its center. He set fire to its contents and while it burned up, he opened his window and seated himself on the sill waiting. Through the open window came the scents of the distant fields, which all the sultry vapors of the city could not quench. The air was full of thundering and the heavy sky compressed the air beneath it.

Soon the charcoal glowed. Ceolfrith sprinkled upon it the incense powder he had compounded. From the center of the circle he turned his face towards the mirror and, fixing his eyes upon the face of the lady, he began with a trembling voice to repeat a powerful incantation. The lady grew pale and then all at once flush. Ceolfrith began a yet stronger conjuration. She hid her fevered face in her hands.

His beloved rose and paced her room seeking and, at length, as if she caught a glimpse of Ceolfrith, her eyes widened. She drew closer to the mirror than ever before. Eyes met eyes. Her expression was enigmatic—tender entreaty mixed with fascination.

Though his heart labored in his throat, Ceolfrith would not allow emotion, good or ill, to turn him from his task. Meeting her gaze, he began the mightiest charm he knew. The lady turned and walked out of the door of her reflected chamber.

A moment later she entered through his.

Forgetting all his precautions, Ceolfrith sprang from the charmed circle and knelt before her. There she stood, the living lady of his passionate visions beside him in a thundery twilight alit in the glow of a magical fire.

"Why," said the lady, with a trembling voice, "did you bring a poor maiden through the rainy streets alone?"

"Because I am dying of love of you," Ceolfrith replied short of breath. He then added in wonderment, "But I only brought you out from the mirror there. Yes?"

"Ah, the mirror!" and she looked up at it and shuddered. "I am a slave while that mirror exists."

She turned to Ceolfrith and said softly, "But do not think I surrendered to the power of your spells. It is not they that drew me to you. It was your longing to see me that beat at the door of my heart until I was forced to yield."

"Could you possibly love me then?" said Ceolfrith, in a voice calm as death, yet almost inarticulate with emotion.

"I do not know," she replied sadly. "I cannot tell what I love or even what love is, for I am bewildered with enchantments. If I were sure you loved me, joy would lay my head on upon your chest and weep. I think you love me, though I do not know . . . "

Ceolfrith rose from his knees.

"I love you as—there are no words—but since I have loved you, there is nothing else." He seized her hand.

She withdrew it.

"No, better not. I am in your power, and therefore I may not yield."

She burst into tears, and kneeling before him in her turn said, "Ceolfrith, if you love me, set me free, even from yourself. Break the mirror."

"And will I have *you* instead of your reflection?"

"That I cannot tell. I do not know. And I will not lie. We may never meet again."

A fierce struggle arose in Ceolfrith's heart. She was in his power. She was fond of him at least. And he could see her whenever he wished. To break the mirror would be to destroy his very life—to banish out of his universe the only glory it possessed. If he annihilated the one window that looked into paradise, the whole world would be but a hellish prison. Not yet pure in love, Ceolfrith hesitated.

With a wail of sorrow the lady rose to her feet. "Ah! you love me not. You do not believe I might care more for your love than even for the freedom I ask. Love cannot be without freedom."

"I will not wait to be willing," cried Ceolfrith. He sprang to the corner where the great sword stood. He groped about to find it for the room had grown very dark with only the embers casting a red glow. At last he seized the sword by the steel scabbard and stood before the mirror but as he heaved a thudding blow, the blade slipped halfway out of the scabbard and the pommel missed the glass and struck the wall above. As it struck, a terrible clap of thunder burst in the very room beside them. Before Ceolfrith could repeat the blow, he fell senseless on the hearth.

WHEN CEOLFRITH CAME TO HIMSELF, he found that the lady and the mirror both had disappeared. Delirium seized him and by it he was kept in bed for weeks.

When at last he recovered his reason, Ceolfrith's first anxiety was the location of the looking-glass. He hoped his beloved had found her way back to safety the way she came. But the mirror was the key that controlled her fate. He knew it was much too heavy for her to carry away and too firmly fixed in the wall for her to remove it.

He remembered the flash and thunder and knew it was a supernatural blow that had struck him down. He surmised his leaving of the mystical circle had exposed him to the vengeance of dark powers. Had the mirror mystically found its way back to its former owner? The question opened up a horrible possibility—by a simple purchase from a crazed shopkeeper, his lady could be delivered up into the power of another man.

Ceolfrith cursed the fact that his beloved, who had prayed to him for freedom, should be at the mercy of another or at the very least exposed again to constant observation. Selfish indecision alone had prevented him from shattering the mirror at once.

Anxiety slowed his recovery, but at length he was able to creep down the steps from his apartment and make his way to the old broker's shop. Though he pretended to be in search of something else, a laughing sneer on the old man's face showed the charade to be useless. The old man knew. But the mirror was not among the items for sale and the shopkeeper would give no information as to its current location. The old curmudgeon feigned the utmost surprise when Ceolfrith, who saw through his counterfeit pity, told him the mirror had been stolen. The old wretch did not care whether or not Ceolfrith believed his act, nor that his former client was coming apart from distress.

All that could be done to begin a search in which it was impossible to ask questions, was to keep ears awake for the remotest hint or clue that might give direction. Ceolfrith abandoned his hermitage and began to accept every social invitation on the chance, however poor, that he might obtain some information. Whether he should see the lady again became a distant second thought. He now sought only her freedom and wandered here and there, like an anxious ghost, pale and haggard. Ceolfrith was gnawed ever at the heart by the thought of what she might be suffering—all because of his self-centered hesitation.

One night, he mingled with a crowd that filled the rooms of one of the most distinguished mansions in the city. He wandered from circle to circle, listening to every stray word that passed him by, hoping for a hint of revelation. He wandered towards some ladies who were talking quietly in a corner and paused. One said to another:

"Have you heard of the strange illness of the Lady von Schaffhausen?"

"Yes, it is very sad for so fine a woman to have such a terrible malady. She has struggled for over a year now."

"I heard she had been better for some weeks, but over the last few days the symptoms returned, more severe than ever. It is altogether inexplicable."

"Isn't there a strange story connected with her illness?"

"I have heard only pieces. But rumor has it that she gave offense to some great-aunt, highly trusted by the family. The old crow, after some incoherent curses, disappeared. The illness followed soon after. But the strangest part of the story is its association with the loss of an antique mirror which disappeared with the aunt . . . "

Here the speaker's voice sank to a whisper, and Ceolfrith, although his very soul sat listening in his ears, could hear no more. He trembled too much to dare to address the women, even if addressing them was advisable. Fearful of attracting attention, and because he could not recover an appearance of calmness, Ceolfrith made his way to the open air. At last, he had the name of his beloved and had heard of her before. But, though he knew where she resided, he still knew not the location of the ghastly mirror whose destruction was his singular goal.

Ceolfrith hoped more unexpected information might come his way and it did the day he returned to the university. On the library steps a question was called out to him, "Have you seen Steinwald lately?"

Ceolfrith, pulled from his thought, gave answer, "No, I have not seen him for some time. He is almost a match for me at the rapier, and I suppose he thinks he needs no more lessons."

"I wonder what has become of him," returned the fellow student, "Last I heard from him he spoke of returning to the broker's den he had visited with you. He said something about going to make a second purchase. It must have been full three weeks ago . . . "

This hint was enough for Ceolfrith. Steinwald was a man of influence among the well-to-do. His reputation was one of reckless habits and fierce passions. The very possibility that the mirror should be in his possession was hell itself to Ceolfrith von Hubert. He must somehow gain access and break the fatal glass but violent or hasty measures would steal from him all chance. There was nothing to do but bide his time.

At length, Ceolfrith heard of a party Steinwald's mother was throwing. The evening of the event, he hastened home and dressed in what finery he had in the hope of mingling with the guests. His confident carriage had granted him entry into such affairs many times before.

MEANWHILE, IN ANOTHER PART OF THE CITY in a lofty, silent chamber lay Ceolfrith's beloved. The comeliness of death seemed frozen upon her face, for her lips were rigid, and her eyelids closed. Her long white hands were crossed over her breast and her shallow breathing did not disturb their repose. The lady's soul was evidently beyond the reach of all who tended her.

The two maids, who sat beside her, spoke in the gentlest tones of subdued sorrow, "She has lain so for an hour."

"This cannot last long, I fear."

"How much thinner she has grown within the last few weeks! If she would only speak, and explain what she suffers, it would be better for her. But she will not tell of her visions and trances when she is awake."

"They say she walks sometimes, and once put the household in a terrible fright by disappearing for a whole hour. She returned drenched with rain, almost dead with exhaustion and fright. But even then she would give no account of what had happened."

A scarcely audible murmur from the yet motionless lips of the lady and startled her attendants. After several attempts to speak, the word "*Ceolfrith!*" burst from her. For a moment she lay still and then with a wild cry, she sprang erect from the couch. Her attendants rose to meet her as she flung her arms forward with clasped and straining hands, eyes wide and flashing. She called with a voice exultant as that of a spirit bursting from a sepulcher, "I am free! I am free! I thank you!"

Sobbing on the couch she fell but just as quickly arose. She paced wildly up and down the room with gestures mingled with delight and anxiety. Turning to her motionless handmaids she called, "Quick, my cloak and hood!" Then more soft and low, "I must go to him. Make haste! You may come with me, if you will."

In another moment all three were in the street, hurrying along towards a bridge on the edge of town. The moon was near her zenith and the avenues almost empty. The lady soon outstripped her maids, and was halfway over the bridge before her attendants reached its footings.

"Are you free, lady? The mirror is broken. Are you free?"

The words were spoken close beside her as she hurried forward. She turned and there, leaning on the embankment in a recess of the bridge, stood Ceolfrith in splendid dress but with a white and quivering face.

"Ceolfrith!—I am free—and am your servant forever. I was coming to you now."

"And I to you, for death made me bold. But I could get no further. Have I atoned at all? Do I love you a little—truly?"

"Ah, I know now that you love me, my Ceolfrith, but why speak of death?"

He did not reply. His hand was pressed against his side. She looked more closely. The blood was welling from between his fingers. She flung her arms around him with a faint bitter wail.

When the maids came upon them, they found their mistress kneeling and cradling a pale dead smiling face.

Appendix 2
What Ciara Was Reading

Bertha and Oswalt[13]

ONCE UPON A TIME THERE LIVED A PRINCESS named Bertha. She was the pride and joy of her parents, King Flauntroy and Queen Matilda. She was so graceful, clever, and lovely that her mother thought of nothing else. Princess Bertha never wore an outfit more than once before the queen replaced it with something prettier. If she so much as smiled at the way a dish tasted, the footman was ordered to bring her ten servings. Everyone said Bertha was the most beautiful, most talented princess in the whole world—except her mother's older sister, Aunt Gertrude, the Duchess of Fogglestone.

Aunt Gertrude had a face as broad as the side of a barn, topped with unruly hair, red as flames. She had one glass eye always pointed in the oddest direction and her one good eye was the color of the mildew that grew beside the latrine. Her face, though as wide as the full moon, barely contained her mouth. Children were always afraid she would eat them up until they saw she had no teeth. Inner

---

13 Aka "Graciosa and Percinet" by Mme. d'Aulnoy (1697).

beauty is what matters but alas, Gertrude was just as ugly on the inside. Fortunately, Aunt Gertrude did not live in the same castle as the king, queen, and princess. Unfortunately, she did live in a neighboring one.

When Princess Bertha was sixteen, her mother took ill and died. She mourned as any daughter would, but King Flauntroy became so melancholy he shut himself up in his palace, not showing his face for a whole year. Concerned for his sanity, the court physicians ordered that the king should go out and amuse himself. For this purpose, a hunting party was arranged. The king had been inactive for so long, and the weather was so hot, that his majesty soon tired. Since the party was passing Fogglestone Castle, the king dismounted and sent a servant to ask for refreshment.

When Duchess Gertrude heard that King Flauntroy had come, she went out to meet him herself and invited him into the cool of her cellar to taste his choice of her ciders. "Sire," she said in the loveliest voice she could muster, "we have Canary Apple, Hermitage Red, Monastery Raisin, sparkling Pomeranian Pomegranate, or St. Julien champagne. Which do you prefer?"

Flauntroy preferred champagne to all other beverages and said so. Duchess Gertrude took up a little hammer and tapped upon a cask twice. But, instead of drink, out came at least a thousand gold crowns.

"I don't understand! What's the meaning of this?" she cried with coy surprise. Then she tapped the next cask, and out came a bushel of silver pieces.

"I just don't know what is going on," cried the duchess, smiling more than before, reaching to twirl a bright unruly lock in her index finger. She went on to the third cask. Tap, tap, and out came such a stream of diamonds and pearls that the ground was covered with them.

"Oh do forgive me, Sire," she cried, "I do not know how or why, but someone has stolen my good wine and put all this rubbish in its place!"

"Rubbish, do you call it, Madam Gertrude?" cried the king. "Why there is enough here to buy ten kingdoms and all the champagne they possess."

Bertha's father noticed neither his thirst nor the heat now. All he could think of was what he might do with such wealth. His fingers itched and he trembled.

Gertrude batted what eyelashes she had and said as demurely as her toothless mouth would allow, "If I were to *marry*, all this treasure would belong to my *husband. He* would know what to do with it. But what do *I*, a simple woman, know of these things?" A giant crocodile tear ran down her plump cheek, "I only wanted to give my lord a cold drink."

The king did not hesitate, but cried joyfully, "Gertrude, marry me! Tomorrow if you like!"

"I make one condition," said the duchess, savoring her first and final moments of courtship in the same split second. "I must have entire control of Princess Bertha, to raise her as I see fit."

"Oh certainly, you shall have your own way. Let us shake hands upon the bargain," said the king, his eyes all aglitter, a man newly fallen in love with the contents of a cellar.

So they shook. Flauntroy even flourished a kiss upon Gertrude's hand as they climbed out of the vault together. The duchess locked the door and gave the key to the king.

WHEN FLAUNTROY GOT BACK to his own castle, Bertha ran out to meet her father. When she asked if he had had good sport, he replied, "I have caught a dove."

Bertha clapped her hands and asked to see the bird, hoping to have it as a pet. So giddy and insistent was she that her father was forced to speak the plain truth, "I met with the Duchess Gertrude and have promised to marry her."

"Dove?" cried Bertha, "You mean a screech owl!"

"Watch your mouth, young lady," said Flauntroy, becoming very cross. "You will behave properly towards her. Now go and make yourself fit to be seen. We are going out to meet my bride-to-be."

The princess trudged to her own room where Nurse Ethel asked the cause of her tears.

"My father is marrying my enemy. The one person in the whole kingdom who does not think I am pretty and kind and charming, my hideous Aunt Gertrude."

"You must remember that you are a princess," answered Ethel, "and make the best of whatever happens. Promise me, do not let the duchess see how much you dislike her."

It was a hard promise but at last, for love of her wise nurse, Bertha consented to being amiable. Ethel dressed her in a robe of pale green and gold brocade, and combed out her long fair hair till it floated round her like a golden mantle. On her head she put a crown of roses and jasmine with emerald leaves. When Ethel was done, Bertha was beautiful in spite of her sadness.

Meanwhile, Duchess Gertrude was also occupied in attiring herself. She put in a cunningly made glass eye in the place of the one that lilted. She gelled her hair until it was tamed and painted her face. She put on a gorgeous robe of lilac satin lined with blue, and a yellow petticoat trimmed with violet ribbons. She had heard that queens always rode into their new dominions so she ordered a horse to be made ready for her.

Ethel was so speedy in her work that Bertha was ready to travel long before her father. To pass the time, she went down all alone through the garden into a little wood.

There she sat upon a mossy bank and began to think. Her thoughts were so doleful that she began to cry once again. She cried for so hard and long that she forgot all about going back to the palace. When she at last looked up there before her stood a handsome page. He was dressed in a green that matched hers, and the cap which he held in his hand was adorned with white plumes. When Bertha looked at him he went down on one knee, and said to her, "Princess, your horse and your father the king await you."

The princess was surprised and delighted at the appearance of the charming page. Thinking he might belong to the household of Gertrude, she inquired, "How long have you been in papa's service?"

"I am not in the service of the king, madam," he answered, "but in yours."

"In mine?" said the princess with surprise. "Then how is it that I have never seen you before?"

"Ah, Princess!" said he, "I have never before dared to present myself to you, but now your father's marriage threatens you with so many dangers. I am Prince Oswalt, of whom you may have heard. I hope to be of use to you in all your difficulties. Will you permit me to accompany you under the disguise of a page? I must confess that I love you and hope that in time I may win your heart."

"Ah, Oswalt!" cried the princess, "Is it really you? I have heard of your wondrous riches and generous gifts. I have wished often to see you. If you will indeed be my friend, I shall not be afraid of what awaits me in the hands of Duchess Gertrude."

The two went back to the palace together, and there Bertha found that Oswalt had brought a beautiful horse for her to ride. She mounted and he led the spirited animal by the bridle. The bonny brown mare was so stunning that when the duchess' mount arrived it looked like an old cart horse in comparison.

King Flauntroy was distracted. He had money on his mind and did not notice the discrepancy in mares nor the new page who was causing a buzz among the servants, especially the maids. When the processions met halfway, the king and princess saluted the duchess who was seated in an open carriage trying in vain to look dignified. Her queenly mount was brought forward for her to ride the rest of the way in the position of consort to the king. But when Gertrude saw Bertha's horse, she cried angrily, "If that *child* is to have a better mare than mine, I will go back to my own castle this very minute. If I am to be queen, I will not be slighted!"

At once, Bertha's father commanded Bertha to dismount. He dismounted himself, bowed, and begged his fiancé's forgiveness, offering her the honor of riding the noble animal that had briefly belonged to his daughter. The Duchess humphed, but without a word scrambled up upon the beautiful horse. There she sat looking like a bundle of laundry. It took eight groomsmen to hold her up and prevent a tumble.

Next, Gertrude grumbled and muttered and threatened until she also had Oswalt as page.

As Oswalt crossed the road to his new assignment, he and the princess exchanged looks, but said not a word. The procession continued in pomp and pageantry, and for a short while the duchess was elated, basking as the center of attention.

But then, the beautiful horse began to plunge and rear and kick. At first Gertrude clung to the saddle but she was very soon thrown off and fell in a heap among the stones and thorns. There the servants found her shaking with fury. Her bonnet was here and her shoes there. Her face was scratched and her fine clothes were covered with mud. Never was a bride-to-be seen in such a dismal plight. She was carried back to the palace, given a warm bath, and put straight to bed. But as soon as she recovered enough to be able to speak, Gertrude began to vent and rage.

Gertrude declared the whole affair was Bertha's fault, accusing the princess of being passive-aggressive and manipulative. "She is trying to get rid of me!" she screeched with accompanying tears. The king seemed unable to answer until Gertrude declared, "If Bertha is not punished, I shall go back to my castle and enjoy my riches by myself!"

At this ultimatum, the King blanched white. He had begun to count on all those barrels of gold and jewels for the fiscal renewal of the kingdom. He hastened to appease the duchess, and told her she might punish Bertha in any way she pleased.

Bertha was summoned by her stepmother-to-be. As she approached, the princess turned pale and trembled. She looked about but could not find Oswalt. If only he knew and would come to my rescue, she thought. As soon as Bertha entered Gertrude's room, she was seized by four brutish women in waiting. All were tall and strong and armed with large bundles of rods. From her sickbed, the duchess commanded the princess be beaten without mercy. Bertha submitted to her fate but then, to her surprise, the beating felt like the striking of peacock feathers. Though the strapping women went on and on until they could no longer raise their arms from their sides, the princess felt no pain. But since the duchess expected her to be black and blue after such a beating, Bertha groaned as if in agony. Hurrying back to her quarters upon her release, she told the whole story to Ethel, who strengthened her with praise and encouragement.

When Ethel slipped out to fetch a little something for Bertha's supper, Prince Oswalt slipped in. Bertha knew her salvation was due to him and she thanked him heartily. They smiled at one another together over the false satisfaction of Bertha's enemies. After advising Bertha to pretend to be in recovery for a few days, and hearing Ethel at the door, Oswalt disappeared as suddenly as he had come.

The Duchess, for her part, was so delighted with the punishment she inflicted that she recovered her own health at twice the speed and then demanded her wedding occur at once in all magnificence. The King did not argue, and they were wed before the sun set.

NOW KING FLAUNTROY KNEW that above all other things his new queen loved to be told that she was beautiful, so he arranged a grand tournament in her honor. All knights in attendance had secret orders to declare, when before the podium, that Gertrude was the most beautiful woman in the world.

Numbers of knights came from far and wide to joust, and the hideous queen sat dressed in great finery in a decorous balcony to watch the contests. Bertha was made to stand at attention behind her. There in the balcony, the princess's loveliness was so conspicuous that the combatants could not keep their eyes off her, but thankfully, the vain queen was certain the admiring glances were for herself. The King either did not notice, or did not care. He was happily counting what freely flowed from the Fogglestone cellar.

During the last grand parade, a young unknown knight, who had won the grand prize, presented himself to the princess instead of the queen and called out for all to hear, "Behold, the Queen of Beauty!" While Bertha had no difficulty in guessing that it was Oswalt, Queen Gertrude did not care who it was that spoke the words, only that the words dared to be uttered. She was so furious she could not speak. When she did recover her voice, Bertha received a torrent of reproaches.

"Who do you think you are! Winking and encouraging knights to flatter your ugly face. I know what you trade in return, proud Princess! I will not bear the duplicity. You will feel my revenge."

"I assure you, Madam," said Bertha, as firmly as she could muster without raising her voice, "that I had nothing to do with his flattery. You, and only you, should be declared Queen of Beauty."

"Ah! you like to jest, Princess of Vanity!" said Gertrude, "but it will be my turn soon!"

Word was brought to King Flauntroy that his daughter was terrorized by his new wife, but he only said, "The queen must do as she sees fit. Her stepdaughter must learn to respect her elders."

When night fell, Gertrude ordered a second-rate carriage, forced Princess Bertha to enter, and commanded it driven away. The horses did not slow their furious pace until they reached a deep forest hundreds of miles from home. The area of the woods was known for its dangerous carnivores and was avoided by all who traveled. To come at night was suicide. But, in spite of Bertha's tears and entreaties, Gertrude's henchmen threw the princess from the carriage and left the forest with more speed than when they came. Driven by terror, the horses needed no prodding to return to the safety of their stables.

Bertha stood quite still at first, bewildered, but when the last sound of the retreating carriage died away she became certain that at any minute she would be eaten by some ferocious beast. She ran aimlessly in every direction. When she finally collapsed exhausted upon the ground she cried out miserably, "Oh, Oswalt! Where are you? Have you forgotten me altogether?"

She had hardly spoken when the trees surrounding her lit up with a golden glow. The radiance was clearer than sunlight and softer than moonlight. At the end of a long avenue of trees opposite her the princess saw a palace of clear crystal. A slight sound behind her made her start and turn around. There stood Oswalt.

"Did I frighten you, Bertha?" he asked. "The palace is my mother's and she bids you welcome." Oswalt whistled for a coach and one approached before the forest stopped ringing with the note. It was drawn by two stags. Once Bertha and Oswalt were aboard, the deer bounded off towards the crystal palace where Oswalt's mother greeted Bertha like she was her very own.

A magnificent banquet was given and Bertha, having exited from the terror and deprivation of the forest and entered into the safety and plenty of the palace, exulted. After supper Oswalt walked with Bertha and his mother on each arm, into a drawing room. There Bertha saw, to her amazement, that the story of her life was represented, frame by frame in watercolors, down to even to the moment when Oswalt found her in the forest. Not only was she loved, she was *known* and loved.

"Your painters are quite diligent," she said, looking at Oswalt.

"They must be," he answered, "I will not have anything forgotten that happens to you."

The princess grew sleepy. Maids put her to bed in a beautiful room and outside her window, musicians lullabied her to sleep. Her dreams were all of mermaids, cool sea waves, and caverns. In these she swam exploring with Oswalt. But her first thought when she awoke was her father, King Flauntroy. As much as she loved the palace and its inhabitants, she could not stay. She must return home. The maids dressed her in a robe designed and hand-sewn by the Queen Mother herself and Bertha was radiant as it flowed from her.

Prince Oswalt's face fell when Bertha told him of her wish to go back home. He begged her to reconsider. He reminded her of the desertion of her father and the evilness of her stepmother. He proposed marriage and confessed his love and desire for her happiness. But Bertha was quite determined to return to what was familiar.

Oswalt persuaded her to stay eight days, which passed too quickly. During that span, the princess grew anxious about what untruths her father might be told about her disappearance. Knowing Prince Oswalt had a way to see from afar, she pressed him. He took her to the top of the highest tower. At the upmost rampart, Oswalt held both of his beloved's hands and pressed his forehead upon hers, eyes closed. Immediately Bertha saw Gertrude speaking with her father, saying, "Your daughter is dead. And she is no great loss. Her casket is closed for her body is badly torn. She shall be buried at once."

Bertha saw that her father believed his daughter to be in the coffin. She saw how the old king cried and would neither eat nor drink. She heard how all the people murmured that Queen Gertrude had killed the princess with her cruelties. Bertha cried out, "Oh, Oswalt! Take me back quickly if you love me."

And so, though Oswalt thought it unwise to return, and it broke his heart to let her go, he gave Bertha her freedom.

"You may not regret losing my company, Bertha," he said sadly, "for I fear that you do not love me well enough. But I foresee that you will more than once regret that you abandoned the happiness of my mother's crystal palace."

Bertha bade farewell to the tender love of the Queen Mother. Oswalt brought the little sledge with the stags, and Bertha mounted beside him. They had traveled less than a hundred yards when a tremendous noise reverberated. Bertha turned back to see the palace of crystal fly into a million splinters. Then, like the spray of a fountain, it vanish.

"Oswalt!" she said, "What has happened? Why is the palace gone?"

"It was built for you and me by my mother," he answered. "But it is a thing of the past since you chose to leave it."

"Will I ever see another?" Bertha wondered aloud.

"Yes, but not until after you are buried," was his quiet reply.

"Do not be angry with me," said Bertha as sweetly as she knew how. "I am suffering from great sorrow."

OSWALT, KNOWING THE CONDITION OF THE KING'S MIND and the tangle of his hasty marriage, gave his beloved the gift of arriving unobserved. Bertha ran up to the great hall where her father was sitting alone. Flauntroy was beyond startled, listening with wide eyes as his daughter told him how Gertrude had abandoned her in the forest and how the casket was buried empty. He immediately had the coffin exhumed and found it just as Bertha said. He kissed his daughter with tears streaming down his eyes and the two enjoyed a single happy supper together. But a servant, hoping for favors, ran and told the wicked queen.

In stormed Gertrude and her husband trembled before his wife. His soul, with what little courage it possessed, had been bought by the riches in the kegs. When Gertrude condemned Bertha as an impostor, the king did not argue. When she had Bertha dragged away he did not defend his only daughter. Stripped of all her finery, Bertha was shut up in a dismal attic room. There she wore a rough cotton frock, wooden shoes, and a little cloth cap. Straw in a corner was her bed, and a bit of black bread each day was her diet. In the confines of the attic, Bertha did indeed regret leaving the crystal palace. She knew she had no right to ask Oswalt for aid.

Gertrude, greatly embittered, sent for reinforcements. An old witch even more malicious than herself arrived, to whom Queen Gertrude made the following request: "I will pay you well to find an impossible task for the fine princess. I wish to sweep away any accusation that I am unjust. Her failure must fall squarely upon her own shoulders."

The witch procured a tangle of thread, three times as big as herself. So delicate was the twine that a breath of air would break it, and so snarled that it was impossible to see the beginning or the end of it.

The queen sent for Bertha, and said to her, "Do you see this entanglement? Set your clumsy fingers to work. If you are a true princess, it will be coiled and smooth by sunset. If not, you are a traitor and will be hung." The door of Bertha's room was slammed shut and locked thrice.

Bertha stood dismayed at the sight of the terrible skein. She turned it over to see where to begin, and saw a thousand threads break. She dropped it and sat down in the middle of the floor beside it crying. "Oh, Oswalt! This fatal tangle will be the death of me. Please forgive me and come to my aid."

Immediately Oswalt entered as if he owned the original keys.

"Here I am, princess. Though you do not love me as you should, I am ever at your service."

She leaned her head upon his shoulder and let out a long sigh. Oswalt but touched the knotted mess and the thread mended itself where it was broken and wound itself as if on an invisible bobbin, smooth as glimmering silk.

The Prince then asked if there was anything else she needed. Bertha shook her head no and stared at the smooth beauty of the task's results. Enamored with his handiwork, she did not notice his arms open to receive an embrace of thankfulness.

Not turning, Bertha complained, "I am so vexed and unhappy here, Oswalt."

"Come with me my beloved," he replied, "and we shall dance upon the hills."

"But suppose you get tired of me?" said Bertha.

A shadow of grief clouded Prince Oswalt's countenance and he left her without another word.

All at once, the wicked queen arrived at the cell door. She cackled to the ladies who followed her, "I'll venture to say that the idle minx has not done anything at all—she prefers to sit with her hands still to keep them soft and uncalloused."

But as soon as the door opened, Bertha presented her stepmother with a large ball of thread in perfect order. The queen was furious. Finding no real fault with Bertha's work, she pretended the thread was soiled. For this imaginary fault she gave Bertha a blow on each cheek. The tender skin of the princess turned from white and pink to green and yellow. The garret was locked once more and Bertha was once more alone.

Gertrude sent for the witch again and demanded a refund for her failure. The witch was aghast but promised she could find something quite unachievable if given another chance. Gertrude grunted giving the slightest of nods.

The witch returned the next day having procured a huge barrel of feathers. Next to the barrel was a cage full of all sorts of birds: nightingales, canaries, goldfinches, linnets, chickadees, parrots, owls, sparrows, doves, cardinals, wrens, and larks. Each sat ashamed, having been plucked clean. The cage and barrel were so large that two footmen struggled to haul them before Queen Gertrude. "Your Majesty," said the witch, "These feathers are all mixed up in such confusion that the birds themselves cannot pick out their own. Tell your precious princess to pick out and lay in separate heaps the feathers of each bird."

Gertrude was delighted, quite sure this task would cause Bertha to despair. She summoned the princess at once. The new task was assigned and the old threat repeated. The feathers were to be sorted by sunset or Bertha faced hanging. The princess set to work at once, but, before she had pulled a dozen feathers from the barrel, she found that it was perfectly impossible to discern one type from another.

"Oh well," she sighed. "The queen wishes to kill me, and if I must die I must. I cannot ask Oswalt to help me again. Anyway, if he really loved me he would not wait till I called him. He would already be here."

"I am here, my Bertha," laughed Oswalt, springing out of the barrel of feathers. His eyes sparkled at the joke of his grand entrance. But his question was serious, "How can you still doubt that I love you with all my heart?"

Bertha stood wide-eyed.

Oswalt inhaled deeply and then let out a mighty sneeze. All the feathers flew about in a tempestuous whirlwind and, just as quickly as the prince had sneezed, they fell to the floor. Every one of them was sorted into neat separate heaps all round the room.

"What should I do without you, Oswalt?" cried Bertha gratefully.

"Come with me my fair one," he replied, "and we shall leap upon the mountains."

"How can you call me fair?" asked Bertha, brushing off her cotton frock and gingerly touching fingertips to bruised cheeks.

Again grief clouded the Prince's countenance, and he left her without another word.

When the wicked queen came at sunset, she was amazed and infuriated to find the task done. However, she complained that the heaps of feathers were not symmetrically arranged, and had the princess beaten until bruises shown all over.

Gertrude screeched at the witch for another failure and demanded a third trial ending in success, or else she would meet the fate intended for Bertha. The witch was terrified and promised to think of another task for Bertha, worse than the two previous.

AT THE END OF THREE DAYS the witch returned again, bringing with her a box.

"Tell your slave," she said to the queen, "to carry this box to whatever destination you please. But she is for no reason to open it. The princess will not be able to resist, and you, Gracious Gertrude, will be satisfied with the result." So Gertrude went to Bertha where she sat in somber silence in the garret and said, "You are free. Only first carry this box to the neighboring castle and place it upon the table in the entranceway. I forbid you, though, to open it and look upon the contents."

The task was so simple that Bertha could hardly believe her ears. She dared to hope a little for a new beginning with her stepmother. She set out at once, wearing her little cap and wooden shoes and the old cotton frock. Even in this disguise the passers-by took note and wondered who she could be. She had not gone far before the heat of the sun and the weight of the box tired her so much that she sat down to rest. Bertha carefully held the box in her lap as she enjoyed the shade of a little wood which grew beside a green meadow. All at once she felt a great craving to open it. What could possibly happen if I did? she asked herself. I should not take anything out. I will only look

And without further hesitation, Bertha lifted the cover.

In a blink, out came swarms of little men and women, no taller than her fingers. They scattered themselves all over the meadow, singing and dancing, and playing the merriest games. At first Bertha was delighted and watched them with much amusement. But eventually, when she wished to go on her way, she found that there was no way to convince the little ones to get back into their box. If Bertha chased them in the meadow they fled into the wood. If she pursued them into the wood they dodged round trees and behind sprigs of moss. It was a great game to them and with peals of elfin laughter again and again they scampered away.

Exhausted, Bertha sat down. In dread she remembered: Gertrude made no threat this time. She promised me my freedom if I succeeded and told me of no consequences if I failed. The omission of a punishment left Bertha terrified. She sat in the great helpless apprehension of the unknown and cried out, "Oswalt, this mess is all my fault. If you can still have mercy for an imprudent princess such as I am, I beg you to come and help me once more."

And once again Oswalt stood before her.

"Hello, my dear Bertha," he said. Then, with raised eyebrows, he added, "I believe you would never think to call on me at all if not for your wicked stepmother. I may owe the evil queen a strange debt."

"Oh Oswalt, I would think of you!" said Bertha, rising to her feet and smiling. "I am not without any gratitude. There are signs I shall love you properly one day."

Oswalt smiled in return. He gave a low, long whistle and all the willful little elves came scrambling back over each other into the box. Next he saw to it that Bertha did not have to walk the rest of the way, for he lifted her into a waiting chariot and accompanied her to the neighboring castle.

When the princess presented herself at the door, and said that Queen Gertrude had ordered her to place the box in the foyer, the governor laughed in her face. "No, no, my little maid," said he, "that is not the place for you. No dirty wooden shoes can step upon this floor."

Bertha begged him to at least give her a written message telling the queen that he had refused to admit her, that she had indeed come and tried to gain entry. This he did, having caught sight of the chariot and driver and finding himself suddenly sobered. Upon her request, Oswalt escorted Bertha back to the wicked queen though he did not take the shortest route. Bertha did not mind that the journey was lengthened. Before they parted, she promised, "Oh sweetest Oswalt, if Gertrude is cruel just one more time I will leave her and my home at once and come to you forever."

Oswalt gave a small half smile but did not reply.

When the queen saw Bertha returning, she fell upon the well-paid witch, pulled her hair, and scratched her face. She would have killed her if witches could be killed. When the princess presented the letter and the box, Gertrude threw both upon the fire without so much as opening either.

Done with the help of witches, the queen had a great hole, as deep as a well, dug in her garden. The top of the hole was covered with a flat stone. She invited her ladies in waiting, among whom she now included Bertha, to go for a walk through the garden on a cool evening. The company paused by the stone.

"I am told that a great treasure lies under that stone. Let us see if we can lift it," suggested the queen.

So they all began to heave and pull. As soon as the stone was lifted high, Gertrude gave the princess a push. She was sent hurtling down to the bottom of the well as the others let the stone fall across the opening once again. Entombed alive, Bertha was now hopeless and sure that not even Oswalt could find her in the heart of the earth.

"I am buried," she said with a shudder. "How I have suffered for lack of trust in my prince. I could never be quite sure that he would not be like other men and tire of me from the moment I gave in and loved him with my whole heart."

As she dried her honest tears a little door opened. Sunshine blazed into the dismal well. With amazing ease she climbed out, almost floating, and found herself passing through a charming unknown garden. Flowers and fruit grew on every side, fountains splashed, and bright birds sang in the branches overhead. Having reached a great avenue of trees, Bertha looked up to see where the road would lead her. There in the distance was another palace of crystal and the Queen Mother and Oswalt were coming out to meet her. Bertha ran to them.

"Princess Bertha," said the queen, "Do not keep my son in suspense any longer. He has suffered great anxiety while you remained under the power of that miserable Gertrude."

The princess bowed before her, rose and kissed her gratefully. "Madam, I shall do whatever you ask of me."

The Queen placed Bertha's hand in the hand of her son. Bertha smiled, turned to Oswalt and said, "You told me that I should not see the crystal palace again until I had been buried. I have been. Here I am to marry you if you still wish it. I love you with all my heart."

Prince Oswalt radiated joy and, lest she change her mind yet again, wed Bertha that very day.

Appendix 3

The Decrepit Old Book on the Windowsill[14]

ONCE UPON A TIME, THERE DWELT IN A LARGE FOREST an old witch woman and three youthful maidens. All three were pleasant and beautiful. The youngest of the three, by the name of Louisa, was also endowed with grace and wisdom. Their hut was so tucked away that no one saw the maidens' beauty except the sun by day and the moon by night.

Meanwhile the vile witch, known to the villagers as old Mrs. Podly, kept the girls busy with work from morning till night, spinning yarn from golden flax. As soon as one distaff was emptied, another took its place, so no rest ever came to the three. The thread was to be woven fine and even and as each spool was finished, it was taken by the old hag and locked up in a secret chamber.

Twice every summer Mrs. Podly would journey away. Before she left, she gave out tasks to fill the time of each maiden for her days of absence. She never told them from where the gold flax came, nor its purpose. She never told

---

14 Aka "The Water-Lily and the Gold-Spinners" from *The Blue Fairy Book*, by Andrew Lang, 1889.

them what became of the golden thread, and she always returned at night while the young women slept.

Every time Mrs. Podly set out on another journey, she would assign each maiden her work, and a warning, "Children, beware your wandering eye. On no account should you ever speak to a man. If such a travesty should occur, your thread's brightness will be no more, and nothing but misfortune and suffering will follow in your footsteps."

The maidens paid no heed to this oft-repeated caution. "How does a golden thread lose brightness?" they laughed, "and what man would journey here?"

Three days had passed since Mrs. Podly's departure when a prince, a charming young man named George, was hunting in the forest. By great misfortune, he found himself separated from his companions and became completely, utterly lost. George searched for his way hour after hour and became so weary he collapsed under a tree. There, in sheer exhaustion, he fell asleep.

The sun was set when he awoke but, sensing danger, he arose and continued his attempt to find his way out of the forest. At last and to his great joy he perceived a narrow foot-path, which he eagerly followed. It led presently to a small hut. There at the door, he saw the three maidens.

As George gave greeting, the two older sisters became frightened and ran, for they remembered the old woman's warning. However, Louisa held her ground. Never before have I seen a man, she thought. I just want one look at him. Her companions frantically gestured for her to come in, but seeing she would not listen, closed the door tight, leaving Louisa alone outside with the prince.

George courteously greeted Louisa, and told her he had lost his way in the forest and was both hungry and weary. The delighted young maiden eagerly shared the bread remaining in her pockets, and for hours the two talked. Louisa was so invested in the conversation with George that she did not once think of Mrs. Podly or her caution. She lingered with him for hours.

Meanwhile the Prince's companions sought Prince George far and wide. At last, they sent two messengers to inform the king that his son had disappeared. The king immediately ordered a regiment of cavalry and infantry to scatter and find him.

For three days the cavalry searched rigorously for Prince George. When at last they found him, he was still sitting by the door of the hut deep in conversation with Louisa. He had been so pleased in the maiden's company that for him it was as if only an hour had passed. George rose to go, promising to return. He expressed in the presence of all the king's men his sincere desire to bring Louisa to his father's court and for them to become husband and wife.

When Prince George had gone, Louisa sat down to her wheel to make up for lost time. She found that her thread was no longer bright and her heart beat violently. She wept remembering Mrs. Podly's warning and dreaded what terrible things might follow. When the old witch returned that night, she knew what happened by the sight of the tarnished thread. She scolded Louisa and shouted that nothing but misery and anguish would fall upon not only her, but also the prince.

Louisa could not rest. She was filled with thoughts of regret, fear, and sadness until she could bear it no longer. She resolved to seek help from her dear George.

SOMEWHERE IN HER CHILDHOOD, long before she came to live with Mrs. Podly, Louisa had been taught the unique ability to speak the tongue of birds. Upon seeing a raven perched upon a pine, she put her skill to use. Softly she spoke to the bird, "Dearest fowl, cleverest of all, swiftest on wing, I beg you for aid though I am unworthy."

"What task does the maiden request of me?" the raven responded.

"Fly away," Louisa said, "until you come upon a town where the king's palace stands. Seek out my dear Prince George and tell him that a great misfortune has overtaken me. My thread has lost its brightness and my elder, Mrs. Podly, has become very angry. I dread the tragedy that might come."

The raven nodded in acceptance and flew away.

Louisa went home and all day she labored to wind up the yarn her elder sisters had made, for Mrs. Podly no longer allowed her to spin.

Towards evening she heard the raven's caw from the pine tree and eagerly hastened to hear an answer. The raven had had good fortune. In the palace garden he had happened upon a wizard's son who shared Louisa's ability of talking with birds. The raven had entrusted the message to him.

Prince George was alarmed at Louisa's situation and took counsel at once with his friends to see about her freedom. He relayed to the raven by way of the wizard's son the following message: "Tell Louisa to be ready on the ninth night, for then I will return and rescue her from that dreadful place."

The raven flew so swiftly that he reached the hut within a single evening. Louisa thanked the bird heartily but told no one of his message.

The ninth night drew near and Louisa's heart was struck with great anxiety. She imagined some mishap would ruin all her hopes. Creeping out of the house, she waited trembling. A little distance from the hut, she at last she heard the muffled tramp of horses. Armed troops appeared, led by Prince George who had prudently marked all the trees beforehand so he could find his way back to Louisa.

George sprang from his horse, lifted Louisa into the saddle, and without a word they began the journey towards his home. The way was made clear by the brightness of the moon.

By the coming of dawn the tongues of fowls loosened, and the trees came alive with their calls. Had the prince known their speech, or if Louisa had listened, the couple would have been spared much sorrow. But they could think only of one another, and it seemed they were out of the woods. The sun shined upon them from the heavens and all seemed well.

The next morning, when Louisa did not come to her work, Mrs. Podly asked where she was. The sisters had been told nothing, but suspected all. Still, for their Louisa's sake, they feigned innocent stupidity. But it was no use. The old witch now sought to punish the fugitives.

Old Mrs. Podly collected various ingredients for enchantment and concocted a mixture of nightshades, adding nine grams of salt, corrupted and bewitched. A curse was created and encapsulated within a ball. The old woman then wound the orb tightly with yarn spun from the mangy fur of stillborn raccoons. That evening, as the sun set, the witch unleashed it before a stiff wind that blew towards the fleeing couple. From the roof of the cottage before a coming gale she cried out—

Whirlwind! Whirlwind! Mother of wind!
Lend thy aid 'gainst they who've sinned!

The Forging of Finnian Ludwell

Cast her from his arms forever,
Deep within the rippling river.

AT MIDDAY THE PRINCE and his men came to a wooden bridge over a deep river. It was so narrow that only one rider could cross at a time. The horse on which George and Louisa rode had reached the peak of the arch as the witch's orb flew by. The steed reared with fright and before anyone could react, Louisa was flung deep into the swift current. George, desperate to save her, started to jump in after, but his men held him back. All signs of Louisa disappeared in the raging current.

George's men took him home but from days to weeks he shut himself up in a secret chamber. He was so torn with sorrow that he neither ate nor drank. So severe was his grief that he became ill to the point of death. The king, in great alarm, summoned all the doctors, wise men, and wizards of his country. But no remedy could be found.

The wizard's son, who had spoken before with the raven, unfortunately made no connection between the odd message and George's illness. But he did go before the king with a plan of action that proved beneficial. He informed the king of an elderly yet sagacious wizard in Finland, "Sire, may your kingdom continue forever, have you heard of Master Bittercress? All the wizards in the throne room combined, no offense to my father mind you, cannot compete with his competent conjuring." Hearing this, the desperate king at once sent a messenger to Finland.

A week passed and instead of a message in return, the elderly wizard himself arrived, flying on the wings of a great wind.

"Honored King," declared Master Bittercress, "Cherchez la femme, which in the tongue of the French means *look for the woman*." The king, though he did not care for the wizard's gauche display of intellect, understood his point. He asked Master Bittercress to continue.

"It is clear what has happened to your son, your majesty.

A curse has snatched away his beloved and with her, his health. His symptoms flew in with the wind, and will only be gone with the wind. Get him up! Get him out! Only the wind blowing upon him will ease his sorrow."

The king with all haste demanded his son go out and stand in the breeze with him that very evening. "George," he begged, "forget the young maiden. There are many beautiful young women in the kingdom. Please just choose one of them."

"How could I?" replied Prince George, "I could never love another! The love inside of me has died, and I might as well too."

But, though his heart had died, the prince did not. Master Bittercress returned to Finland satisfied, reputation intact.

NEARLY A YEAR PASSED before Prince George's long rides in the woods brought him again to the bridge, the very bridge where he lost Louisa. George stood at the edge in silence as he looked down into the rushing water. Then he began to weep bitterly. His tears flowed with no end. He bargained in the midst of his loneliness. He would gladly give everything he possessed away to have her breathing, happy, alive.

At that moment he heard a voice singing, but looking around, he saw no one. Before he could dismiss it as illusion, again he heard—

> *Alas! Corrupt and all forsaken,*
> *That I should lie forever here!*
> *And yet, no thought was ever taken*
> *To free his bride, his love so dear.*

The prince jumped from his stallion and looked about. He thought perhaps someone was under the bridge, hiding, playing a cold trick on him. But lying on his belly and looking under, he saw no one.

Yet he did notice a yellow water-lily floating in the current, half hidden by its broad leaves. Its beauty charmed and comforted him. George turned on his back and stared into the overarching trees, his horse having left to graze beneath them. The blue sky filled him with the hope of hearing more.

Again the voice sang—

Alas! Corrupt and all forsaken,
That I should lie forever here!
And yet, no thought was ever taken
The bride he says he loves so dear.

George remembered the gold-spinners and wondered what they might know. If I ride back to the hut, he thought, perhaps Louisa's sisters could explain the song to me?

WITH GREAT HASTE PRINCE GEORGE SPURRED HIS HORSE on, feeling more hope than had been his in several months. Finally, he found the two maidens at the fountain that flowed behind their hut. Before they could rush inside, he frantically descended from his horse and told them of their sister's fate. He begged them to show mercy and explain the mysterious song if they were able.

The two maidens loved their sister more than they feared the witch. Familiar with the ways of magic, they knew what had befallen her—she was the beautiful water-lily submerged under the bridge. She was not dead, but enchanted. Mrs. Podly's magic orb had flown past and transformed her from flesh and blood to vines and stems.

The witch being gone, the sisters invited George to stay the night. But before he slept, the eldest baked him cake with purified herbs and insisted he consume every crumb. He dreamed that night he was in the forest and understood the tongue of the birds. Rather than tweets and chirps he heard complex communication all around him. At breakfast he told the maidens of his dream.

"It was the herbs in the cake," admitted the second-born. "Now you will understand the birds while you are awake as well. Listen closely, they are full of wisdom and by them you will know what to do next."

Prince George departed refreshed and encouraged, promising he would return after recovering Louisa to deliver them both from their bondage.

As George rode along he could understand the dialogue of the birds that flew above. One particular conversation between a thrush and a magpie caught his ear.

"Are men stupid or do they suffer from a disability?!" tweeted the magpie, "They cannot understand the simplest concept! A year has passed since the maiden shrunk to a plant, and every day she sings so ear-bleedingly loud. One would think she'd be heard by now but no one does anything. Her former finance rode over the trusses just a few days ago, he even heard her singing, but to no avail. He is as stupid as the rest."

"Every bad thing that ever happened to that poor girl has a direct connection to that idiot prince," answered the thrush. "I bet my beak she remains a flower forever, for none seem to think it wise to consult a second time with Master Bittercress."

After hearing this, the prince knew that he had to get a message conveyed to Finland, somehow. Knowing the swallows might find long sticks for their nesting aplenty up north, the prince tried his first stuttering words in swallow-ese, "Excuse me, kind friends!" he cried. "If you happen to be heading north, could you perhaps bring a message to Finland?"

"How quaint that you should try out our language," responded the swallows, flattered, "quite polite, quite progressive of you. We accept your request."

The prince smiled and said, "Take a thousand thankful greetings to Master Bittercress, and ask him for direction on how one might change a maiden, who is currently a beautiful flower, to her beautiful original form." The swallows agreed and flew away, and the prince rode on to the bridge. There he waited, hoping to hear again the water-lily's song.

However, days passed and he heard nothing but the rushing of the water and the moaning of the wind. At last, out of supplies, he rode home with disappointment. He sat in the palace garden and wondered if the swallows had forgotten his message. Looking up he saw an eagle descending, round and round it wafted down, until it perched upon a nearby tree.

George stared at it expectantly and was not disappointed, "The wizard Master Bittercress greets you," the great bird called out. "He bids me to instruct you thus: Go to the river and smear yourself all over with mud, then say, 'I shall be crustacean from flesh and blood.' Once you are transformed, plunge boldly into the water, swim close to the water-lily's roots. Loosen them from the mud and reeds, fasten your claws upon them, and rise with them to the surface. Together you must drift with the current until you come to a mountain alder tree on the left bank. Near it is a large stone. Climb upon the stone with the lily, face the wind, and declare—

> *Together drowned*
> *To past lives dead*
> *Together bound*
> *Forever wed*

Upon chanting these words, you both will be restored to your original forms."

The prince was at first hesitant. He was not used to seeing the ways of magic, much less participating in them. A passing crow had landed and was listening in. He cawed out an unasked-for opinion, "Why do you hesitate? Do you think Master Bittercress is wrong? Have the birds ever deceived you? No they haven't. We have no reason to lie to you or make a fool of you. Defecation on your belongings is the extent of our pranks. Go quickly and relieve your maiden of her tears."

Death is the worst outcome that could befall me, thought George, and death is better than the endless sorrow I now suffer.

PRINCE GEORGE MOUNTED HIS HORSE and rode to the bridge. Again he heard the water-lily's cry. Without hesitation he stripped, smeared himself with mud, and declared, "I shall be crustacean from flesh and blood," and plunged into the river. The water hissed in his ears, then all was silent. He swam up to the plant and, as prompted by the eagle, began to loosen its roots.

The roots were fixed firmly in the mud, but being a crab allowed George the use of claws. At last the pair rose to the surface and the current carried the couple gently down the stream. George kept a sharp lookout for the mountain alder, soon saw the sought-for tree, and scrambled out upon the stone.

With all the elocution possessed by a lipless crustacean, he sang out—

Together drowned
To past lives dead
Together bound
Forever wed

George found himself once more a human prince. Even better, after a year of sorrow and mourning, he found beside him a human Louisa. She was as beautiful as he remembered and wore a pale yellow robe, sparkling with jewels. Free but exhausted, Louisa collapsed into George's arms.

WHEN THE COUPLE REACHED THE BRIDGE where the prince had left his horse, the steed was nowhere to be seen. Though it seemed that he had been a crab only a few hours, the two had floated upon the water for ten days. George and Louisa wondered how they would ever reach the palace.

The King and Queen wept for their son, whom they had mourned as dead. But great was their rejoicing when George entered, leading Louisa by the hand. The occasional kind farmer's cart had carried them along, and at last all was well.

A week later they were joined together in a beautiful wedding. For weeks, feasting and merry-making permeated the kingdom.

Just beginning their happily-ever-after, George and Louisa were nestled in each other's arms in the pagoda of the palace garden when in flew the crow. "You ungrateful pond scum!" he cawed, "have you forgotten the two poor maidens who helped you at your time of distress? You promised to return and free them! Must they spin gold flax forever under the tyranny of that hag? All *three* of the maidens are princesses, not just Louisa. All three were kidnapped quite young, and *you* stop at freeing only one?! Poison is her fittest punishment for the witch who enslaves the beauty and skill of others."

And with his frightful speech completed, the crow flew away cawing as he went. Prince George, greatly shamed, kissed his bride and set out at once.

On his way, the sisters met him. Dreams had predicted his coming and they had made ready. Knowing the greediness of Mrs. Podly, they knew she would never free them. Knowing her bottomless hunger for more, the two sisters cooked a cake containing cyanide from crushed fruit seeds. They left it on a table where Mrs. Podly was sure to see it, and she consumed every crumb. By the next morning, she was prostrate on the floor, lifeless.

Prince George returned to the hut with the sisters and helped bury the old woman. Together they discovered the secret chamber where they found fifty wagon-loads of golden flax and finely wound thread.

Prince George, Princess Louisa, and her two siblings lived the rest of their lives happily, in good health, and in high spirits.

About the Author

According to an ancient sage, there are five reasons a man writes:

1. to assist his memory
2. to help others
3. to injure certain people
4. to show off
5. out of necessity.

Prufrock stories fall mainly into category five. For reasons known only his therapist, Prufrock needs to dust off and rewrite MacDonald. Perhaps reason number two will prove true as well—so if you are helped, please stuff the P.O. Box full of encouragement.

The negativity associated with reasons three and four is held at bay by the fact that the story arc does not belong to Prufrock. Any intended injury is aimed at MacDonald's enemies, and they are long dead. The pride of showing off is likewise avoided. All kudos, in the end, belong to George.

As for assisting his memory, Prufrock does not remember what caused him to write out this little essay in the first place . . . something his editor was asking for . . .

A.J. Prufrock

About the Illustrator

AFTER LOSING HER FAMILY'S FORTUNE to a cryptocurrency scam, Molly Kantz spent the next decade of her life as a wandering soul. Without a penny to her name she hitchhiked across North America, surviving on what little could be earned shining shoes, sweeping floors, serenading passers-by on her portable theremin, and . . . most notably . . . selling drawings.

It was then that A.J Prufrock found her. Molly was discovered sitting on the front stoop of a Dairy Queen, sketching surprisingly competent figure studies upon a motel notepad. After a long conversation, and the signing of a forty-page contract, the newly-proclaimed professional was relocated to a small cottage on Prufrock's estate. Now she works as a full-time illustrator, specializing in digital art and whatever form of traditional art her patron can afford to purchase from her.